Land of Milk and Honey

WILLIAM TAYLOR

Land of Milk and Honey

 HarperCollins*Publishers*

For my very good friend Johannes Luettgen

The author gratefully acknowledges the assistance of Creative New Zealand in the writing of this novel. Additional work on the manuscript was done in 2003 during the time the author was Writer-in-Residence at Whakatane Intermediate School, and this assistance is similarly appreciated.

National Library of New Zealand Cataloguing-in-Publication Data

Taylor, William, 1938-
Land of milk and honey / William Taylor.
ISBN 1-86950-549-2
I. Title.
NZ823.2—dc 22

First published 2005
HarperCollins*Publishers (NewZealand) Limited*
P.O. Box 1, Auckland

ISBN 186950 549 2

Cover design by Darren Holt, HarperCollins Design Studio
Typesetting by Janine Brougham
Printed by Griffin Press, Australia, on 50 gsm Bulky News

Today

Curiosity had attracted most of those who turned out for the auction of the property. Nosy parkers and rubberneckers out for an afternoon's free entertainment. A small gaggle of men in suits were there to do their best to ensure the property realised at least a reasonable return, while the few who had turned out to bid were praying the place went for a song. A soft and warm autumn breeze sang through the branches of a stand of old macrocarpa.

The owner of the farm, aging, if not truly old, observed the goings-on from the sideline — sullen, silent for the most part, and sunk in the knowledge that the sale was unlikely to let him off the financial hooks of those who held the mortgage. He wasn't here from choice; the auction had been forced upon him. His flushed face and flabby bulk gave hint of a life of over-indulgence. Piggy, darting eyes, well sunk in fat, spoke of bad temper.

Another man, also aging, presented in stark contrast to the other. Slim, straight of back, he also stood quietly on the edge of the small gathering, as far from the flabby individual as possible. With him were a young man and a young woman.

'We've got used to you taking us to some strange places, Grandad,' said the young woman. 'But why here?' She shivered, despite the warmth. 'This place gives me the creeps.'

'Yeah, Grandad,' said the young man. 'All the times we've

5

stayed with you, we've never been out this way before.'

'Indulge an old man,' said their grandfather, without smiling.

'Why? Something wrong with you? Losing your marbles at long last? Is that it?'

'You're not even old, Grandad,' said his grand-daughter.

'Depends on your definition of old,' her brother grinned.

'Just remind me to take you on for a set or two of tennis when we get home.' This time the older man did smile.

'That doesn't count, because I always let you beat me,' his grandson laughed. 'Don't want to put a dent in your ego and, besides, Grandma Maisie would be pissed off if you croaked from a heart attack if I really let you have it.'

'Nonsense, you little chicken,' said his grandfather. 'Now shut up. The circus is about to start,' and the grey eyes that had so often laughed at these two took on a hard glint.

There were few bidders for this ragged remnant of a once-prosperous farm. The productive areas that had long ago formed part of the whole had been flogged off over the years. All that was left was a dilapidated old farmhouse, a few crumbling outbuildings, and somewhere around seventy hectares of swampy, neglected land. At best it might appeal to the owners of neighbouring farms anxious to add to the size of their own spreads.

The pantomime played out in fewer than ten minutes. Open-mouthed and wide-eyed, the young man turned to his grandfather in sheer disbelief. 'Why, Grandad? Why the hell have you bought this dump?'

His sister smiled. 'I think you can take your pick, Mack. Retirement hobby farm? Investment property? Change of lifestyle? Grandma Maisie will love it out here.' She laughed.

'She'll be here all by herself,' said her brother. 'She'll have shot Grandad first.'

'Guess to your heart's content,' their grandfather grinned, giving each a quick hug. 'Think I'd better go and sign a few papers and write a cheque.'

'Well, there's our inheritance gone,' Mack shook his head. 'Right down the gurgler. Sure the old memory's OK these days, Grandad? Ever find yourself getting lost and forgetting things? Things like who you are?'

'Why, Grandad?' his granddaughter asked again, as the three of them wandered around the place the old man had just bought. 'What are you going to do with it?'

'Give it away.'

'Very kind of you, Grandad,' said Mack. 'But I don't really want to be a farmer. Can I flog it off again? Nice of you to think of me, but cash would have been OK. Easier, too.'

'You!' his grandfather chuckled. 'You want a farm? Cash? Damn well work for them.' He turned to his granddaughter. 'It's mine for just as long as it takes to give it away. It's going lock, stock and barrel to the wetlands people.' He pointed. 'Bush reserve up there . . . and down over there, see that ocean of flax? Swamp, wetland reserve. This block links the two. I'm giving it on the understanding that it be allowed to revert to bush, swamp, whatever.'

'The house? Buildings?'

'Will be gone just as soon as a bulldozer does a spot of long-overdue work.' The hard grey eyes had lost any trace of humour.

The young man looked into his grandfather's eyes, a glimmer of a smile on his good-natured face. 'I don't think you've lost your memory, Grandad. I was just joking about that before. There's something about this place, isn't there? Why else did you bring Emma and me with you today? Yeah. There's something about this place. You going to tell us?'

The trio rounded a corner and the old man paused. 'Milking shed . . .' He sighed. 'Well, once it was. Come on, you two. Let's go. I've seen enough. More than enough.' He turned to walk back towards the house. Their way was barred.

'Long last, eh, Doc? Got what you wanted now? Reckon it took you a while. Guess you think you've done for me this time, Pongo.' The speech was slurred, the fat red face bloated, blood-engorged, angry. He carried a bottle, punctuating his speech with frequent gulps. 'What do you say to that? What've you been telling these two, eh? Telling them what you got up to down here all them years back? Bet you haven't told 'em the half of it. Bet you haven't told 'em the good bits.' A sneer and a snarl.

'Get out of the way, Pearson. In fact, get off the property. It's my bloody property now!' Each old man glared at the other.

'Come on, Grandad,' the girl took hold of her grandfather's arm. 'Let's go.'

'Yeah. Go on. Run for it, Pongo. You did it before, when you couldn't take it. Now do it again,' the fat man jeered.

'You don't speak to my grandfather like that!'

'Forget it, Mack.' Suddenly his grandfather laughed. 'Leave him be. Come on you two.' He pushed the grotesque, bottle-waving and blustering barrier to one side and the three of them left the place.

1947

. . . unto a land flowing with
milk and honey . . .

(Exodus 3:8)

I

The train stopped. The guard bustled along the aisle of the near-empty carriage, tapped the boy on the shoulder and said, 'Come on lad, we're here. This is it, so get a move on. Haven't got all day.'

'I must get my suitcase,' said the boy.

'It's with the luggage in the guard's van. Come on, now. You hop out and I'll get it for you.' A not unkindly voice. 'Be careful getting out, lad. It's quite a step. Hope for your sake someone turns up to meet you before too long.' The man looked from the carriage window. 'Don't like the look of this weather and you'll find next to no shelter here.' He looked down into the boy's pinched, pale and worried face. 'Don't you fret yourself, now. Reckon someone will be along in a minute, if they're not already here. Come on now, let's be having you.'

The guard was wrong. There was no one waiting for him. The place was deserted. He was right, however, about the weather. He was right, too, about the lack of shelter. There wasn't much to the station. The structure was minimal — just about big enough to carry the name of the place — a name the boy couldn't pronounce. The 'station' was just a rail-siding, with little more than a sealed strip and a bench propping up the name-bearing sign. Soon the boy was soaked. He took his reading glasses out of his pocket and put them on in the hope of seeing better and peered into the persistent rain.

Time passed. He didn't know how long he'd been waiting. An hour? Maybe more. He waited. There was nothing else he could do. On one side of the make-shift platform the railway line ran off into the rain as far as his eyes could see in either direction. On the other side of the platform a gravel road ran parallel to the rail track. There was no traffic on either rail or road. No sign of life whatsoever. No other building other than this ramshackle, skeletal station.

He waited, huddling for shelter. Very soon even his heavy Harris tweed jacket was soaked through. Soon, too, the wetness on his cheeks wasn't only from the falling rain.

This boy was patient. He waited. Then, growing tired of inactivity, he picked up his case and walked off along the road into the foggy gloom. A hundred yards, maybe a little more. Maybe there was something else hiding in the fog. Turning to look back he could no longer see the bench. Alarmed at losing sight of this one cheerless but familiar feature so quickly, he retraced his steps and huddled down again. The late afternoon darkened and fear added to his sodden misery.

'My word and you'll be the lucky one, then,' the woman in Wellington had said. 'Milk and butter and cream and eggs! Fresh meat,' the woman licked her lips, eyes glinting at the thought. She chuckled. 'Put a bit of padding on those bones of yours in no time flat,' and she had pinched his cheek. 'Look in a mirror in a couple of months and you won't know yourself . . . The lucky one, indeed.'

'What about our Janice?' he had asked.

'Who?'

'Our Janice. My little sister. What about her, Miss?'

'Goodness gracious me! Don't you be bothering your head about

11

your sister. She'll be as right as rain wherever it is she's going.' The woman consulted a list. 'Just er . . . not too sure at the moment . . .'

'My father said . . .' he began.

The woman didn't give him a chance. 'Whatever it was your father said, boy, must have been said a long time ago and with little knowledge of the er . . . state of things . . . er . . . .' The chuckle was well gone. 'Your sister will be fine.'

'But . . .'

'She'll be fine. D'you hear me? D'you understand? Now, then, no more of this nonsense. There are them as would give eye-teeth for the chance you're getting. A farmer's life for you, young fellow-me-lad. You'll be living off the fat of the land and the pig's back, and don't you forget to show how grateful you are!'

The gloom faded still further into eerie darkness. Eventually the rain thinned into a chill and misty drizzle. The boy was shivering now and clutching to him the only thing of substance he had with him; his suitcase. Cold, wet, hungry and, increasingly, scared. Where was he? Where was this place that was no place at all? What was he to do if no one came? Had the train stopped in the wrong place? Would there be another train? Where would he go on another train if one came and stopped at this odd spot with a name he couldn't read? His shivering grew into an involuntary shaking and his slight body was so convulsed he forced himself to stand, jumping up and down in an effort to get his body under some sort of control. It didn't work and he slumped down again onto his suitcase.

A noise? He started. What was it? An animal? At first a faint whine

. . . then growing . . . A train? Something. Not an animal. It must be a train. He stood and peered in the direction of the sound. And then a light . . . lights. It was a vehicle, not a train. He stepped towards the approaching, still-distant light and the lights, now two of them, grew. Headlights. He began to wave.

Heedless of any possible danger he moved from the platform and onto what he knew was the roadway. His waving became frantic, more frantic the closer the weaving headlights came. And they were weaving unsteadily, and not very quickly, towards where he stood. The vehicle, a truck, snaked to a stop.

For a moment there was nothing other than the grumbling sound of an old and uncertain engine. The sound of a window being wound down and a head poked through. 'You the boy?' A rough voice.

The boy, tentative now, approached and peered into the cab of the truck. The fumes of the old vehicle didn't fully mask those of another unmistakable substance — beer. 'Yes,' he said, more uncertain. 'I'm a boy.'

'I can see you're a bloody boy! What's your name?'

'Jake.'

'That's it, Dad. That's him,' another voice. 'Sure as hell no one else around here.' A rough laugh. 'Looks half-drowned. Looks like a stinking skinned rabbit.' More laughter.

'Come on. Haven't got all day — or all night.' Another laugh. 'Get your gear.'

'I'll just get my suitcase,' said the boy.

'Geez, Dad, right little pom we've got here. Listen to him. Can't understand a word he says.'

He collected his suitcase and returned to stand by the cab of the truck. For a moment nothing was said. And then he asked, 'Please may I get in?'

13

Loud laughter from inside. 'No room,' said the younger of the two. 'You think we want a bloody drowned rat in here making us all wet?'

'Up on the back, kid. That's where you ride — not that you'll have time to be riding anywhere. Get used to it,' said the older man.

'Chuck your bag in and climb up after it, Pommie,' said the younger voice. Comfy enough for the likes of you. Even got an old dead ewe in there to rest on. Get to know her — you'll be skinning her in the morning. Her and her dead lamb.' Both voices laughed. 'If you're lucky you'll get to eat her as well. First bit of decent meat you'll have had for God knows how long.' And the two of them continued to laugh as he struggled frantically to clamber onto the deck of the truck, worried even this cold comfort would take off without him. The driver, the older man, revved the engine a couple of times and their amusement grew as the boy became more desperate in his efforts. They fuelled their fun at his expense, passing between them and taking turns drinking from a bottle of beer.

The drive was long, the road was rough, the driver was drunk and, after a moment of revulsion, the boy was thankful for the presence of the dead sheep. The first and only soft thing he'd found to cling to since arriving in this gloomy place. By leaning back into the carcass the worst jolts were partly absorbed. He spread his legs and clung into the sheep's fleece.

It was very dark. The only light came from the truck headlights, fitfully piercing the black distance. At least the rain had stopped.

'What time do you call this, then? You're late,' snapped the woman.

'This here's the wife. Mrs Pearson to you, boy. I'm Mr Pearson. That's what you'll be calling us. Understand?'

'You're late,' the woman said again.

'You can blame him, Mum. Bloody train was late. It's all his fault,' and the young man winked at the older.

'Don't you swear in front of me,' said the woman.

'Sorry, Mum. But it's all his fault. And you can call me Mr Pearson, too, kid. No one's ever called me that before. Reckon there's got to be a first time and I like the sound of it.'

'Show him where he's to bunk down, Darcy. Then bring him back to the kitchen. Mum and me, we'll lay down the ins and outs of what he's to do. Got the meal ready, woman? Could eat a bloody horse and chase the rider.'

'Better see if he's got dry things in that bag of his, son. Don't want the little blighter sick on us the minute he gets here. God knows what germs he's brought with him so don't you be going too close,' said Mrs Pearson.

'No fear of that, Mum.' Darcy Pearson grinned. 'Come on, kid.'

'Thank you,' said Jake, for no particular reason.

'Thank you who?'

'Thank you er . . . Mr Pearson.'

'That's better.' Darcy grinned again. 'Come on.'

'And don't be long if you want to eat,' said his mother.

The room was very small. Just big enough to hold the furnishings, though there were scant furnishings for it to hold. A bed and a box. The bed was half-size, little more than a child's cot, with three or four old grey blankets tossed over a stained mattress. The wooden box might have been chair or table or cupboard. There was a small window, broken, over which a sugar sack had been nailed. The floor

15

was almost whole — other than where floorboards had rotted. The walls and ceiling were of corrugated iron. There was one luxury — a naked light bulb. The room was well-ventilated. Wind whistled in through the holes in the floor as well as through the broken window-pane.

Darcy Pearson stood in the doorway, his grin broader than ever. He was enjoying himself. He smoked. 'You smoke?' he asked Jake.

'Yes I have . . . well, sometimes,' said Jake.

'Well don't think you're getting my smokes, Pom. How old are you?'

'I'm fourteen,' said Jake.

'Jesus!' exclaimed Darcy. 'You don't look it. How old do you reckon I am?'

'I don't know,' said Jake, standing by the bed and looking up into the face of the other. He shivered slightly, and not from the cold.

'Seventeen. Well, just about,' he leered, and did his best to blow smoke into Jake's face. 'Reckon I could wring your scrawny neck if I wanted. There's not much of it.' Darcy Pearson flexed a muscle, winked, and grinned some more. 'There'd be no one to miss you and it might be fun to give it a try. The old lady said to get dry clothes on. Come on. Get 'em out.'

'I haven't got much more with me.' Jake struggled to open his suitcase.

'You better bloody have or my mum'll be whacking your skinny bum. She's a powerful whacker, let me tell you. Not that she'd dare do it to me any more so she's looking for a new customer.' He sniggered. 'Reckon you won't be putting up much of a fight when she gets stuck in.'

The contents of Jake's case were little drier than the clothes he wore. He found what he could and hesitated, looking up at his tormentor.

The grin became a full-bellied chuckle. 'Get changed, Pom. I'm starving for a feed. Come on. Strip right off. Get a move on.'

'Um . . . er . . .'

'Come on. Let's see what you're made of. Now!' Darcy Pearson lit another cigarette and blew out a stream of smoke. 'Whew! Could break your back as well as wring your flaming neck. Talk about a scrawny, scraggy little rooster! Boy oh boy, I'm going to have fun with you! Dammit, I can hardly wait.' He chuckled to himself.

Still chuckling, he led his victim towards the lights of the house, stopped for a moment and pointed. 'That there's the dunny,' he announced.

'The what?'

A coarse laugh. 'The shit-house. If you don't want to piss or shit your pants that's where you do it. It's a bloody hole in the ground,' and he turned to face Jake, grasping the boy's arm in a strong hand. 'And remember this,' he hissed. 'You get on my goat and you'll end up down there.'

'On your . . . goat?'

'You know what I mean,' grunted Darcy.

II

He would get used to the food. In the end it would be the least of his troubles. 'You'll be living off the fat of the land and the pig's back,' the woman had said when he got on the train. Well, he seldom knew what he was eating, nor did he give it much thought, but one thing was for sure, he doubted that what he ate was any respectable portion of a pig or of any other beast, for that matter. Even during the worst years of the war, with Mum and Dad and Janice, then with Gran, before she died, even the year at the convent after Mum had been blown to smithereens, he'd never tasted food worse than that served up by Mrs Pearson.

He ate to stay alive — and that was the sum of it. Porridge in the morning, after milking — porridge that was either grey and watery or the consistency of mixed cement. Never halfway between. As much milk as he wanted, and that was the only good thing. Bread, generally dry, for lunch. Bread with a skerrick of butter or a scrape of dripping. Supper — tea, as the Pearsons called it — varied slightly. Sometimes it was grey stew served with potatoes. Sometimes it would be grey stew served with bullet-hard little dough-balls, dumplings. Sometimes it might be grey stew served with slabs of the dry bread.

The woman would serve it at the bench and her husband, son and Jake would take their plates from her. There would be a sneer on her face as if challenging any one of them to make comment, to say something. None of them did.

Jake ate the slops and came back for more. He never knew if the others ate everything. He didn't eat with the family.

'You'll have your food in the wash-house. There's a bench out there. Never had the worker eat with us, not ever. It wouldn't be nice and it's just not done,' Mrs Pearson had ordered. 'Rinse your plate under the tap when you've finished, leave it on the bench and bring it back in next time. Understand?'

He understood. He was to understand the lay of this land very quickly. The farm belonged to the woman, not her husband. She was the boss. Not that she did anything, either outside or inside the home. The old man ran the place.

That first night would be the only occasion during his time with the Pearsons that Jake would be inside the house proper for longer than it took to get his food. He stood. The Pearsons sat around the kitchen table. Six hard eyes measured him up.

'We've been good enough to give a home to a poor war orphan . . .'

'I'm not an orphan,' said Jake.

'Speak when you're spoken to, lad,' said Mrs Pearson.

'My father is alive,' he said, 'I'm not an orphan.'

'As far as we're concerned, you're an orphan. That's what we told the authorities we wanted, out of the goodness of our hearts. Whatever it is you've left behind in the old country you'll soon forget, and a good thing, too.'

'Yeah, Pommie, you'll be too busy to be thinking of anything but work.' Darcy Pearson grinned. 'That's what you're here for.'

'He knows that,' Mrs Pearson glared at her son. Mr Pearson, tired after a hard day's work, leaned back in his chair and snored

19

slightly. 'Wake up, Clarrie. We're talking to the boy,' she said loudly and her husband snorted himself awake.

'What about me going to school?' asked Jake.

'School? What d'you mean, school?'

'Do you hear that, Mum? Thinks he's going to school. Geez, have we got a surprise for him.' Darcy Pearson chuckled happily.

'To the best of my knowledge, you're fourteen years of age, not far off fifteen. There's no school for you, boy. You're here as our farm worker and that's what you'll be doing,' said Mrs Pearson. 'By the time you've settled in here and learnt the ropes, you'd be of age to leave and no one would mind.'

'But . . .'

'But nothing. Let that be an end to it. Goodness, gracious, whatever next?' The woman barked out a laugh. 'We don't have our worker going to school. We asked for a good strong boy for farm work . . .'

'Yeah, and look what we got, a skinny little runty weasel,' said Darcy, continuing to enjoy himself.

Mr Pearson grunted. 'Not to worry. We'll get our money's worth out of the little blighter, or my name's not Clarrie Pearson.'

'Before I was so rudely interrupted . . .' Mrs Pearson started again. 'Let's put an end to this school nonsense. You're here as a worker, boy, nothing more and nothing less, even though our Darcy tells me you didn't bring suitable work clothes. I'm willing to concede the authorities might not have told you, what with things as they are in the mother country . . .'

'They told me I'd be going to school in New Zealand,' said Jake. 'That's what they told my Dad and they told me.'

At which point Mr Pearson stood, scratched his belly and looked down on Jake, then lifted his hand and swiped him across the head.

'You'll learn one lesson quick, lad, and that's don't answer the wife back. Get that into your thick skull. Understand?'

Darcy Pearson giggled happily. 'Don't you worry, Dad. I'll be helping him understand. Hell's bells, I'm looking forward to the responsibility.' He grinned at Jake, this time with menace in his smile.

Jake swayed on his feet. A wave of nausea hit him in the gut and it took what meagre strength he had left to stay upright. Above all, he was tired. He was very tired. Exhausted. This day had brought him much too much. Even the scant comfort offered by the scraps of grey blanket and the stained mattress in his room out the back would be better than this. But they hadn't finished with him.

'Let that be a lesson to you,' Mrs Pearson stared at him. 'And now, as I was saying . . . We'll give you working clothes Darcy has grown out of and you'll meet the cost of these by not drawing your wages for the first month you're here. Normally, we're generous with our worker, but you're inexperienced so you can't expect normal rates. You'll be paid five shillings per week less two-and-sixpence for your board and lodging. That'll leave you with half a crown. Of course you'll meet the cost of any damages, breakages, whatever . . . I hope for your sake you're not too clumsy.' Another bark of a laugh.

'If the wife has finished with you, get to your room,' said her husband. 'Up at daybreak. Your first lesson in milking. Thank your lucky stars there's only a handful in milk so far. Have you ever seen a cow, lad?'

'I've lived in the country,' Jake whispered. 'Just for a little while with my Gran . . . when the bombing was bad.'

'Not our country,' said Darcy Pearson. 'Reckon you haven't seen cows anything like ours.'

'And now, get away to bed with you,' said the woman. 'Wash your face and hands at the tub in the wash-house. Off you go. You do right by me and Mr Pearson and we'll do right by you. And make sure you don't waste the electric. Five minutes, no more, and you turn out the light, or I'll be down there to take out the light bulb.'

'Would you like me to help him back to his room, Mum? Seeing as it's his first time and he might lose his way?' Darcy licked his lips expectantly.

'No need for that, son,' said his mother, firmly.

Jake found his own way back to his room and turned on the light. For a moment he sat on the side of the bed, numb with tiredness. He stood, weaving a little on his feet. He shook out the rough grey blankets, wrapped them around him without taking off his clothing, pulled the light cord, found the bed and lay down. For a brief moment he thought of his little sister, Janice. For a briefer moment he saw his father, and remembered the wry grin, the quick hug and the quick goodbye. For a fleeting second he pictured his mother, and then with eyes tight shut he put her picture from his mind.

Jake was too exhausted to feel anything, too exhausted to think anything. He fell into a deep and dreamless sleep.

III

Jake worked. Jake learnt. He worked hard and he learnt quickly. It was just as well — most lessons were accompanied by a clip around his ear, a boot to his backside and a string of curses from either Pearson — father and son. Jake suffered at the hands, feet and mouths of both, and both were at their most foul-tempered in the early, dark dawns. Above all he learnt to keep his mouth shut. It was made quite clear to him that, given a very short time to learn the ropes, the work would be largely his, overseen by Darcy and not the old man; a prospect that filled Jake with dread.

Old Pearson he could live with, tolerate, and even understand. The younger Pearson was something else again. The boy spotted quickly that Darcy was obliged to take almost as much from his father as he was. Nowhere as much physical abuse but much of the verbal torrent was directed at them both. Jake knew instinctively that once the old man left the overseeing in his son's hands his life would be even less worth living. The looks of pure hatred Darcy shot in his direction whenever his father was making him the butt of his ill-temper added to Jake's fear, more so in the knowledge that he would soon be at his mercy.

Darcy Pearson delighted in brutality, took pleasure in the infliction of pain and was at his happiest when making the life of some other living creature an absolute misery. He took care around his father and their herd of milking cows. While the old man was not averse to giving the tail of a reluctant cow a sharp and painful twist, he had enough good farming sense to know that a tormented beast isn't going to produce a good quota of milk. Milk was money. At least when his father was around, Darcy made sure he followed suit. He reserved his vengeful energies for when the old man wasn't there or when a likely prospect didn't count for much. Those that counted least on this farm were the bobby calves, redundant off-spring of the milking cows. All of the bull calves and many of the heifers, separated from their mothers a day or two after birth and unceremoniously dragged to the farm gate; caged, collected and carted off to slaughter. Darcy Pearson was an expert at making the short life of a bobby calf a pain-filled, terrifying hell.

Jake stood, white-faced, trembling, as Darcy dealt with a calf that hadn't wanted to be caught. 'Teach you a lesson, useless little blighter,' snarled Darcy, as his new-born victim bellowed satisfactorily. 'You don't take shit from these suckers,' Darcy turned to Jake. 'What's the matter with you? Feeling sorry for it?' The look that suddenly dawned on Darcy's handsome face was one of ultimate satisfaction — he'd discovered a prime method of tormenting the younger boy. He booted the new-born calf again, lit himself a cigarette and grinned at Jake. 'Feeling sorry for it, eh? Come on,' he wheedled, softly. 'Have some fun. You can have some bloody great fun with these little sods.'

'No,' said Jake. 'It's only a little baby.'

'Useless bastard. Look!' and he yanked up a leg of his victim. 'See its nuts? Deserves everything it's getting.' Grinning widely, he slowly twisted its leg so that the animal cried again. 'No use to us. Next to worthless.'

'Don't. Please don't hurt him,' said Jake. 'It's not his fault and he's only a little baby.'

Darcy mimed a throat slitting. 'Yeah,' he jeered. 'And that's what's going to happen to this little baby. Come on. You have a go. Boot the bugger.'

'I will not,' said Jake.

'Aw, go on,' grinned Darcy.

'Let me take it down to the gate,' said Jake. 'I'll put it in the pen down at the gate.'

'Gee, kid, can't have that. You've done enough for the day. You can leave it to me. I'm going to play footie with it all the way down the drive. Wait till you meet my mate, Gary, he's from town. He's even better than me with 'em. Gary sure knows how to have a bit of fun with a bloody bobby-calf,' Darcy laughed. 'By the time good old Gary's worked 'em over, the buggers don't know their arse from their elbow.'

Jake gulped. 'I don't mind taking it to the gate and putting it in the pen.'

Darcy lit himself another cigarette and grinned a smile of fake sincerity at Jake. 'No, I feel like giving it a bit of help all on my own. Come on, useless. Get a move on.' He used his boot on the calf again. 'Move it!'

Most of the time Jake knew he couldn't concern himself about the treatment of new-born calves and their mothers at the hands of the Pearsons. He knew he must keep his mind on the simple act of surviving in this harsh place where, he figured, he counted for little more than a bobby calf and, quite likely, a whole lot less than a bobby calf's mother. Not that there was much time for thinking about anything other than getting through each day.

The farm made a good living for the Pearson family. Swampy, and not the very best of dairying land it was, nevertheless, big enough to support a herd of seventy cows. Clarrie Pearson had a reputation as a hard man, a hard-drinking man, and a reasonable farmer. Before most of the smaller dairying units in the district had thought of it, the Pearsons had installed milking-machines and, in many ways, the cowshed was better than the family home.

One day followed another and the Pearson farm became Jake's only world. He thought little about where he had come from. Occasionally he would think of his father and would wonder, very briefly, how he was getting on, if he had managed to find a job; jobs were scarce for one-legged men. More seldom still he thought of his little sister, Janice. He would shrug, almost indifferently, and send up a sort of prayer that she had ended up somewhere other than on a farm and with people who were the absolute opposite of the Pearsons.

'You must write every week from your new land of milk and honey,' his father had said. 'When you have time from sitting in all that sun they say they have out there and you're big and fat from all that good food.'

A new land of milk and honey? One thing was right, Jake would think; there was plenty of milk. Maybe one day he would find some honey. Resolutely, he would put thoughts of home from his mind. Above all he would close his mind from picturing his mother and the sight of her pottering around the little two-up-two-down they'd called home until the dreadful day they were bombed and half the street obliterated. Jake didn't want to remember her touch, the soft and sweet smell of her, the sound of her voice as she called him or Janice in from the street. Deep within himself he knew there were some things that were better left unremembered — at least for now.

Just occasionally he would wonder about the others who had come out with him to this new land, that sometimes funny and sometimes sad collection of others, like himself and Janice, being sent to better lives. Not that it really paid to think too much about the few good times they'd shared on the long six-week sea voyage to paradise.

Not much time for thinking at all when you slaved seven days a week for a bowl of porridge, a slab or two of dry bread and a plate of grey stew. Not much time at all when you only had five minutes of electric light to shove another wad of damp newspaper into another hole in the corrugated iron that the rain had found to trickle through. A moment or two, sometimes, just before you went to sleep to wonder just when the half-crown weekly pay might start and you could hide it away, hoard it, save it in order to somehow get yourself out of this hell-hole.

Jake wasn't religious but he did take to muttering fragments of the Lord's Prayer, remembered from school, from another world. 'Our Father who art in heaven, or is it which art, it doesn't matter . . . Hallowed be thy name and let your Kingdom come and deliver us from all evil for thine is the Kingdom and dear God in heaven get me out and deliver me from this bloody place!' and, as an afterthought. 'Help the poor bloody cows, too. Thank you kindly, amen.'

The dairy herd controlled his life, from the moment he walked out in the dim, damp light each morning, opening gates and herding the beasts along the track they knew. If he liked anything at all about this place, it was the cows. The only time he spoke voluntarily was to the beasts. He hadn't been worried about their size and had sensed, right from the beginning, that the cows were the only benign, docile presence on the property. He called them all by the same name. 'Come on Big Brown Eyes, and don't you worry, I won't twist your old tail,' and he would tap one on the rump. 'Don't you be lookin' at me, Big Brown Eyes, and you get a move on before I get it in the neck and you, too,' to another. 'Do you have to shit right on my foot, Big Brown Eyes? I'll thank you not to do that ever again and don't you forget it! It wasn't me sent your little baby to the knacker's yard and you mark my words, Big Brown Eyes, your little one is better off down wherever it is. Well, I think it might be up in heaven by now. If calves go to heaven and I think they should.' And he would yard them, bale them, wash their rear-ends and udders and have the right number ready before his bosses turned up to make the lives of the lot of them, cows and boy, as miserable as they could.

He learnt to separate the cream from the milk and haul the full cream cans to the stand down at the gate, one can at a time, using a sled built for the purpose. He stoked the fire that heated the water needed to scour the cream cans and the milking equipment, frequently scalding himself in the process. He sloshed through odorous oceans of cow effluent with scarcely a thought. He grew quicker, more adept — at both work and keeping out of the way of the hands and feet of old Pearson. No one thanked him for his efforts. The only signal that he was getting better was that he got more work to do and the other two did less. The day arrived when Clarrie Pearson didn't turn up for the morning milking.

'Well, well, well, well, well, Mister Pongo. Just you and me, now. Isn't that going to be fun? Well, for me it is. I've been looking forward to this,' Darcy Pearson announced. 'I'm your boss now, and you'll do exactly what I tell you. Right? Now get to bloody work, Pongo!' He grinned happily as his boot connected with Jake's backside. The milking shed world was now his oyster and he planned to make the most of it. For Darcy this was seventh heaven.

Jake's nightmare deepened.

IV

He should have been warned. He shouldn't have allowed himself to be sucked in so easily, so readily. Never before had Darcy offered to haul the cream cans to the road. This time he did. 'I'll do it, mate. You just hose down the shit and I'll come back and check you've done it properly. Don't want the old man in a worse temper than usual when he checks up, do we?' Darcy smiled, speaking softly in a tone of sweet consideration and reason.

'OK.' Jake didn't look this strange gift-horse closely enough in the mouth.

When Darcy returned, he appeared satisfied. He took out his cigarettes, lit one for himself and then offered the pack to Jake. 'Go on. You can have one, Pongo, but don't expect them all the time.'

'No thank you,' said Jake.

'Thought you told me you smoked?'

'Only a little bit.'

'Well you can make it a little bit more now. Go on. You've earned it. You just help yourself.'

Jake did. He lit up and drew in the smoke, felt dizzy and coughed. 'I haven't had one for a long time.' In spite of an empty stomach, he enjoyed the smoke and the brief moment of strange familiarity with Darcy. 'Not for quite a long while,' he added.

'I can tell. But don't you worry about it,' said Darcy, smiling.

'Come on through here,' he nodded towards the separator room. 'Got an even better surprise for you through here. Big treat, and all for you. Oh, you're going to love it.'

Jake heard the door close behind him and the turning of a key in a lock. 'What . . .' he turned, looked up into Darcy's grinning face. Tricked. Tricked and trapped. Easy game for a young man of Darcy Pearson's devious skills.

'Said I got a little treat for you,' he nodded. 'You're really going to enjoy this. We both are.'

On the concrete floor was a cardboard box. The contents were fully apparent; a litter of half a dozen squirming, crawling and mewling kittens, about four or five weeks old.

Jake knelt down. 'Kittens,' he said, and stretched out a finger to stroke one.

'My word, you're a bright one. Yes, indeed. Six of the little bastards, all ready and waiting.'

'Waiting for what?' he said dumbly, emptily. But Jake already knew.

'Waiting for you to come along and give them a good home? No, not that, Pongo. These dear little kitties are waiting for you to kill them, you stupid little runt. And guess what? That's exactly what you're going to do while I watch. Torture them and kill them.' Darcy was thoroughly enjoying himself, a broad, self-satisfied smile never leaving his face. He folded his arms and leaned against the door. 'You're going to kill them. Every last one,' and happily drawing on his cigarette, he blew a splendid smoke ring.

'Where's their mother?' Numb now.

'God knows. Probably getting some old tom up her so she can make some more. Come on, Pongo. Get to work. I'm going to enjoy this.'

'I'm not going to kill the kittens,' said Jake, firmly.

'Yes you are.'

'No I'm not. You can kill me first but I'm not going to kill them. Go on. Kill me.'

'I'm not going to kill you. Well, not yet, anyway.' Darcy stretched. 'Don't get me wrong. I'd like to, but not when I can get this sort of fun out of you first. Tell you what, I'll let you do them any way you like. I just want to see you do it.'

'No. I won't.'

'Yes you will. And do you want to know why? I'll tell you, because I'm a nice bloke. You don't do them, I will, and I'm going to torture every one of those little kitties every which slow way you could ever dream of — and you're going to be here with me while I do it and see it all. Believe me, I'm an expert cat killer. Understand?'

Jake got it. 'Please,' he begged. 'Give them to me. I'll look after them. I . . . I'll give them some milk. I will. Please, Mr Pearson, I can't kill them. I've never killed anything.'

Darcy smiled down at him. 'Aw, poor kid. Haven't you? You don't know what fun you've been missing. Who knows, Pongo, you might enjoy it,' and he picked up a kitten. 'Here little kitty, kitty, kitty. What'll I do to you, eh?' he said tenderly, holding the little thing up to his face and blowing a plume of smoke directly into its tiny eyes.

'No.'

'I think I'll slowly break your . . .'

'I'll do it!' said Jake, yelling. 'I'll kill them for you!'

'No, I feel like doing it myself now,' and Darcy twisted the neck of the small and struggling creature until it broke.

Jake howled at him. 'I'll do it, I'll do it! Let me do it. Please, I'll kill them.'

'Go on,' Darcy said softly. 'Do it, then. I knew you'd want to do it once you'd seen what fun it was.'

Jake breathed hard. He sweated, gritted his teeth, felt bile, phlegm in his throat. He picked up the first kitten, closed his eyes, breathed even harder. Quickly, very quickly, he took it by the back legs and with all his strength bashed its head onto the concrete floor. He repeated the action four more times. 'They're dead,' he said dully. 'Let me go.'

'Bet you enjoyed it,' said Darcy Pearson. 'Here, mate. Have another smoke and we'll go and see if we can find some more. Next lot we find, you just make sure you take a bit more time to do it. Oh, I could see in your face how much you loved doing it.'

Jake looked at him. 'Yes. You're right. I did like it. It was good. Now I've got to go. Please open the door. I've got to go to the dunny.'

Jake retched out his empty stomach and his heart. He wiped his hands on his overalls trying to rid himself of the feel of those small warm bundles of struggling fur. Tried to wipe from his mind the sight of six pathetic kitten bodies with lifeless eyes. 'Please forgive me, dear God, because I had to do it. It was better for them that I did it. You have to believe me, God. It was better that I did it.'

Darcy Pearson had not quite extracted every ounce of personal pleasure from Jake's agony. 'Boy oh boy, Dad,' he said, piling porridge into his bowl. 'You should've seen what old Pongo did to a litter of kittens he cornered over in the shed. Worse than me, any day.'

'I didn't want . . . he made me . . .'

Old Pearson slapped Jake hard on the back. 'Getting into our farm ways, eh, Pom?' and he guffawed a hoarse laugh. 'There's another couple of litters over in the hay barn. The two of you can sort them out, too. Damn strays everywhere. Breeding bad as rabbits.'

'Yeah, Dad. We will. We'll get them together, won't we, Pongo? Bet you can't wait.' Darcy turned to Jake and nudged him with his elbow.

'If he has time to be playing around with cats he's got time for more work,' said Mrs Pearson. 'Ragwort is starting to come through in those top paddocks. You can get to work on the end of a grubber before it gets any bigger and starts to spoil the milk.'

Whatever ragwort might be, Jake didn't care. Whatever a grubber was, he guessed he'd find out soon enough. Whatever both of them were, he knew it would mean more work for him. He filled his bowl with porridge and went through to the wash-house where at least he was rid of the Pearsons for a few minutes. Regardless of the sick feeling that would not leave his gut, he ate every last scrap.

He saw the tiny black shadow scurry along the wall of his room and under his bed. At first he thought it was a mouse or a rat, neither of which now worried him. Then he saw the small black shadow again. It was neither rat nor mouse. It was a kitten.

'Come on. Here, kitty.' He knelt down and peered under his bed. A tiny hiss came from a corner. 'Here, kitty, kitty.' It came to him. 'Where did you come from? Did he put you in here?' Jake shivered, stood, went to the door, checked. No one there. 'I think you could be . . . I guess you are . . . one that got away from him. Come on, I won't hurt you.' Then the sick feeling thudded back into his gut. 'Well, I don't want to hurt you . . .' He picked it up in gentle hands. So gentle. 'Oh, you funny little thing,' he said, as the kitten started to suck one of his fingers. 'That's not a tit, dummy. Won't get anything from that.' It went on sucking. 'You stupid little kitty. You're sucking at the hand that murdered your poor brothers and sisters . . .

'Maybe I should kill you, too. Right now. It would kinder than if that bastard gets you and sucks you in with his big smile. Now I'm a bastard, too, but you don't know that. I'm no better than him. Not really. But, you know what? I can't do any more cat killing, not now. You're OK with me . . . Better turn out the light before she screams. You'n me can go to bed and you just pray that I don't squash you flat in the night and don't squawk for food because there isn't any. I'll try and get you some milk in the morning, though God only knows how I'm going to do that! I just hope I can keep you alive . . .

'You've got to go under the floor in the daytime 'cos if you don't, the bastard'll get you. I know what I'm going to call you. You're going to be Little Black Sambo. My mam read that to me when I was little . . . And I'm sorry for what I did to your brothers and sisters . . . but I guess you don't know about that,' Jake looked at the kitten. Little Black Sambo was fast asleep.

Presently, so was Jake, but not before remembering back to when he had a mother who read to him. For a moment or two he thought of her.

V

'This came in the post for you last week,' Mrs Pearson handed Jake an envelope. 'I suppose you better have it, although I must say it's a cheek on the part of the authorities to think they can expect me to deliver your letters.' She didn't specify which authorities. 'It's only out of the goodness of my heart I'm letting you have it. Not that it says much.' Jake reached for his letter. 'What d'you say?'

'Thank you very much, Mrs Pearson,' muttered Jake.

'I would have thought someone living in the old country would know the King's English better than your father seems to,' she sniffed. 'It would seem he doesn't miss you too much.'

Jake saw his letter had been opened. He guessed it had been read by all three Pearsons. He said nothing more and shoved the letter in his pocket. 'Thank you,' he said again.

'Aren't you going to read it?'

'I haven't got my glasses, Mrs Pearson. I'll read it later.'

'I can read it for you,' she smirked.

'I'll read it later,' he repeated.

'Please yourself.' She wiped the smirk from her face with a loud sniff.

The letter burnt a hole in his pocket but he wouldn't give her, her husband or her son the pleasure of further invading what scrap of private world was left to him.

He knew the letter wouldn't say much. He knew the limits of his father's ability. It wouldn't matter what was written. It would have been hard labour indeed, with God only knew which neighbour or friend being called in to give a hand with the spelling, addressing the envelope and, quite likely, making sure the stamp was stuck the right way up!

> *My dear son Jacob*
>
> *How are you. I am well. It is getting cold even if it is still said to be summer and it's not. How goes it with you in your new land. Is there a lot of milk and honey ha ha. I hope you be good for the good folks who give you a good place. You must let me know and right a letter soon so we know. I miss you more than we can say but one day we will see. You are in a best place.*
>
> *The leg is coming on and I do well with it the wood one that is. Hop hop ha ha. When it gets me down I have a beer ha ha. Your old man can still get to fox and grapes hop hop.*
>
> *Yours truly*
> *Your loving father Jim*

Over and over and over again, Jake turned his letter in his hand while Little Black Sambo played with the envelope. He read his letter ten times. He read it twenty times. He heard his father's laugh. Hop hop ha ha! Even at the very worst of times, what a laugh. And then, for better or for worse, there was his mother, brushing Janny's hair and knotting a scrap of pink ribbon into a little blonde top-knot . . .

That night Jake cried himself to sleep.

She was in a good mood. 'Mr Pearson and me will be away for three days for the weekend. Darcy will be in charge and running things and you'll do as he says at all times and make sure you pull your weight.'

'Bet I have to do it all, Mum,' said Darcy. 'Can't see why I can't come, too.'

'With just about the whole herd in milk there's no way you can be spared, son,' said his mother. 'Besides, your father'n me need a break and you shouldn't begrudge us a day or two for your cousin's wedding. I've said you can have Gary come and stay to keep you company. There's a big pot of braised beef and onions,' she pointed to a saucepan on the coal range. 'Get the boy to hot it up when you're ready.'

'You'll have a damn sight better time than going to some tomfool wedding, boy,' growled his father. 'And I've promised to leave you a dozen.'

'Geez, Dad. That's not enough. Could you make it two?' Darcy wheedled. 'Please, Dad.'

'Don't want you and that fool Gary drunk as lords. You've got work to do.'

'Don't you worry, Dad. I'll make sure Pongo here pulls his weight better than ever, just as Mum says.' Darcy grinned at Jake, winked. 'That's going to be the best part of it.' And then, more quietly and out of earshot of his parents, 'Gary'n me have got a few surprises up our sleeves for the runty pom.'

Jake shivered.

'Quite our own little royal wedding it's going to be,' Mrs Pearson got back on track. 'All in the same year as Her Royal Highness. Such a pity Pamela isn't able to wait. Did you ever see the royal family, boy?' she turned to Jake. 'Not that I suppose they'd ever bother about your ordinary bits of England. The little princesses, Elizabeth? Little Margaret Rose? I only wish I'd had a daughter.'

'No,' said Jake. 'No, Mrs Pearson. I've never seen any of them.'

'As I thought.'

'The King came to Coventry after one lot of bombing, and Queen Elizabeth,' said Jake.

'Poor man. And so brave,' said Mrs Pearson.

'But we didn't see him when he came.'

'Well, I should think he had better things to do,' said Mrs Pearson.

'Gary's bringing his motorbike. Thought we'd go shoot a few rabbits up the outcrops,' said Darcy.

'Plenty of 'em up there,' said his father. 'Give the devils hell.'

'And now the young Elizabeth getting married,' said Mrs Pearson, finally helping herself to the stew.

'Thought her name was Pammy,' said Mr Pearson.

'She means the princess, Dad,' said Darcy. 'Pammy's the cousin who's getting married.

'Waste of bloody time, if you ask me,' said his father. 'You be careful with those rifles.'

'Thought we'd use old Pongo digging out the rabbit holes so we can get the little buggers, too,' said Darcy.

'Good idea,' said his father.

Mrs Pearson turned to Jake. 'And you make sure you behave yourself and do whatever Darcy says.'

'He'll be doing what he's told, Mum. You know you can trust me,' said Darcy.

'Yes. Well, that's what your father and I are doing. Treating you like a responsible grown-up. No high jinks and nonsense.' She shook her head. Three days is the longest we've ever left you. Not that it's quite three days. Daddy and me will be leaving tomorrow lunchtime, Friday, and back by late afternoon on Sunday. Now come on, come on. Must get on with my ironing.'

Jake finally got his stew and took it to the wash-house. As ever, he ate automatically, neither relishing nor even tasting the food. It was a dry bread night and he wiped his plate clean down to the last drop of tasteless gravy. His mind was far away from the simple act of fuelling himself. His mind ranged over the grim prospects offered by the next three days and the agonies his tormentor had in store for him. Of one thing he was absolutely sure — Darcy Pearson would not be leaving him alone!

VI

It was heaven and it was bliss. Jake had almost a full day without
any of them. More than worth the hard morning labour of polishing
their car to within an inch of its life! Indeed, Jake enjoyed the change
from dull routine and waxed and elbow-greased the dark red, pre-
war Chevrolet to a gleaming finish that even Mrs Pearson found
hard to fault. 'It'll do,' she had grunted. This was the nearest she'd
ever come to a word of praise. 'The bride's mother will be riding in
it and I will most certainly not see my side of the family let down
even if they haven't got much of a car to call their own.'

Clearly the wedding of Pamela, the niece, was an occasion of
some importance. It was the first time since he'd arrived at the farm
that he'd seen them use the car. So far, the old farm truck had served
their every transport need, from Mrs Pearson's weekly shopping trip
into the town Jake had never seen, to Mr Pearson's almost daily two
or three hours in the pub.

'Just don't you forget, boy, to pull your weight and do as Darcy
says,' she cautioned yet again. 'You're here to work, not lounge
around eating us out of house and home. Come along, Darcy. If you
want a ride to town to meet up with Gary get a move on. Dad and
me are just about late.' She nodded at Jake. 'And you get out and get
on with that ragwort, boy. We'll be checking Sunday afternoon you
haven't been shirking.'

What a bonus! The three of them gone — even if the worst of the three would be back far too soon. In how long? An hour? Two hours?

Jake stood in the driveway as the car drove off and out onto the road and away. A smile spread across his face. At the top of his voice he yelled out after the fast disappearing vehicle, 'Bugger your bloody ragwort!'

He went into the kitchen, cut himself a large slice of bread, found butter and jam in the safe, spread both very thickly on the doorstep of bread. He took his morning tea back to his room and found Little Black Sambo. Together they sat outside in the sun and enjoyed the feast. Well, the kitten didn't sit for too long. Jake returned to the kitchen, made himself a sizeable bread lunch and, as insurance, tucked into his pocket a couple more slices and a crust or two still lying there from the day before. Next best thing to Christmas, he thought to himself.

Jake's holiday lasted for almost a day because Darcy Pearson didn't come home until late on Saturday morning. Not quite a holiday, of course. Would have been more of a holiday if Jake had been given some idea of how long Darcy was going to be away. It was most certainly a working holiday. With just about the whole herd in full milk it meant that most of Jake's time was spent in the milking shed. He knew what to do. For weeks, now, he'd been doing the lion's share of the labour and, back-breaking, exhausting as it was, the very simple fact of not having to keep an eye on the whereabouts of Darcy Pearson meant that for two whole milkings he could relax, let his guard down and have more serious conversations with Big Brown Eyes — numbers one through to sixty-three!

But all good things come to an end, and they came to an end for Jake at lunchtime, Saturday, with the arrival home of Darcy, accompanied by his good mate, Gary. Gary and Jake hadn't met before but Gary was clearly looking forward to the event. 'This ya bloody pom, Darce. He's a weed, eh? Old Hitler sure starved them poms.'

Gary was not a weed. Pleasant of face, big, blond, blue-eyed, thick-set and very thick of mind, at six foot he was a couple of inches taller than Darcy Pearson. Close friends since their very first days at school, the two shared similar interests, most particularly the enjoyment they found in inflicting misery on anything — human, animal or bird — smaller or weaker than themselves. Darcy was the leader and Gary his very willing follower. 'What we gonna do to 'im? When can we start?' he asked pleasantly, after de-capping with strong white teeth the first of the two dozen bottles of beer left for them by Mr Pearson. 'You said we could have us some good fun. You promised. Otherwise we coulda stayed in town, 'cept for the beer.' This was a long speech for Gary, whose abilities were slightly over-taxed in his job as apprentice motor mechanic. He gargled down a good quarter of the bottle of beer and passed it to Darcy. 'Got any smokes?'

'You've got your own,' said Darcy.

'Aw, geez,' said Gary, 'have I?' He patted his clothing. 'Oh, yeah. I do,' He lit one and smoked enthusiastically for a minute or two.

'I've had my lunch,' said Jake.

'He's had his lunch,' said Gary, 'That's nice, eh? Please, Darce, can I do 'im now?'

'Like how?' Darcy was being difficult. A few too many bottles of beer the night before had taken a slight but headachy toll.

'I dunno,' said Gary, wrinkling his brow and thinking very hard. 'Yeah!' Inspiration struck. 'Stick him down ya dunny? Be good fun, eh?'

42

'Look,' Darcy said, patiently, and as if to a small child. 'My old man says it doesn't matter a shit what I do to the pongo . . .'

'The pongo! That's a good one,' said Gary, grinning, smoking, lounging casually in the doorway so the object of their debate couldn't escape. 'Pongo! Stink! Now I geddit,' he giggled.

Darcy sighed. 'Just shut up for a minute, and listen. My old man says he doesn't give a shit what sort of hard time I give the pom but we have to remember one thing . . .'

'What's the one thing to remember, Darce?'

Darcy sighed again. Sometimes his friend was just a little too much to bear. 'If we knock him up too much, my old man says he'll be good for nothing, and guess who'd have to do all the work?'

'Dunno,' Gary look sorely puzzled. 'Who?'

'Like me, Dumbo.'

'Don' call me Dumbo,' said Gary. 'Yeah. I geddit,' Gary scratched his head. 'Couldn't you get another one? Another pongo?'

Darcy Pearson had learnt a valuable lesson in farm economics at the knee of his father. 'Farm workers don't grow on trees these days . . . Not seeing it's after the war, and all. There's next to no one looking for work these days. Even useless shits like the pongo sure as hell don't grow on trees.'

'No they don't,' said Gary, helpfully. 'They wouldn't, would they? Grow on trees, that is. So what you mean is,' he gradually gathered his wits and spoke quite slowly. 'We can't do nuthin' to 'im.'

'Didn't say that,' said Darcy, grinning. 'There's things we can do to the bugger.'

'Right. Gotcha,' said Gary, shaking his blond, curly mop. 'Like what?'

Jake, waiting patiently for the blow to fall, breathed a very tiny inward sigh of relief. It was comforting to know he was unlikely to

43

be killed outright or, indeed, maimed for life or drowned down the dunny. His good sense, however, was fully alert to a wide variety of other less permanent but very painful probabilities.

'You just wait and see. I've got a few good things lined up for him. But, for now, you and me will have another couple of beers and then take your bike and go up the outcrops and kill us some rabbits. I feel a deep and powerful need to kill something. What d'you reckon? Then, don't forget we're going down the hall for the tennis club dance and we've got to get spruced up. That's tonight, remember? We'll take the beers and hide them in the bushes out the back so the old ladies don't know and tell Mum. Come on. Let's go and give those rabbits hell.'

'Yeah. OK,' said Gary, happily. 'Might kill somethin' else as well, eh Darce?'

'And don't you worry,' Darcy comforted his friend. 'I got plans for the pongo. It'll be good, you'll see.'

'What are they?'

'Use your brain, Dumbo,'

'Don' call me Dumbo.'

'Can't tell you now with him listening,' Darcy shook his head again.

'Yeah, Pongo,' Gary spoke to Jake for the first time. 'You stop snoopin' and spyin' on what good blokes say. Go on, ya bugger. Get out!' And he and Darcy spent a pleasant five minutes tripping up Jake every time the boy tried to leave the room.

'And start getting those cows in,' Darcy yelled after him.

Tired? He was always tired. Aching? He often ached. Bruised? Quite frequently. What could he do to escape from this prison? This thought increasingly occupied his waking hours. They couldn't keep him a prisoner. Could they? Well, there were no bars on this prison. But what could he do? What could be done to him if he simply walked out that gate, down the road to . . . where?

Jake scarcely knew where he was. Somewhere in the heart of this country that could not all be, surely, as bad as this corner they'd found for him? Where was he? If he got caught, what then? If they stuck him in a real prison it couldn't be all that much worse than this place. Hard labour. Well, he was now fully trained for that. Send him home? No. They wouldn't do that — much too much to hope for!

What about Little Black Sambo? What about him? Did the cat matter? Not all that much. The cat would take its chances. It would either live or die. Sheer chance, a fluke indeed, that the black kitten hadn't been spotted already. Some sixth sense seemed to tell the kitten to stay out of the way, live under the floor of his room during waking hours, not follow him around. Maybe Little Black Sambo was a survivor.

Was there any point in escape? Commonsense told him it was unlikely he would be sent to prison just for walking out of this hell-hole. But why bother? It was probably no better and no worse for him, here, than it was for the others, wherever they were, who had crossed the oceans of the wide world with him.

He milked the cows. Separated the cream. Sent the skim milk down the long chute to the pens of pigs that fattened on the stuff. Stored the cream in the cool room for the following morning's pick-up. Cleaned up. Back-breaking work for his slight frame. Only one good thing on this afternoon and evening; he hadn't had to put up with the attentions of Darcy Pearson and his good mate, Gary.

As Jake trudged down the race to close gates after the long-gone cows, he wondered what it was that Darcy and Gary had in store for him. Well, at least there was only one day left for them to put

Darcy's plan into action. Jake made sure he didn't go to the house for his dinner until he heard the motorbike take off and away down the drive to the tennis club dance at the local hall.

A restless night.

Jake tossed and turned, slightly feverish in his apprehension that at any moment the axe might fall. At sometime after midnight he came wide awake as he heard the motorbike come up the driveway to the farmhouse. He was fully dressed and had dozed. They wouldn't take him unaware. He pulled back the sack covering the broken windowpane and watched, alert, as the two revellers dismounted and staggered towards the back door. They were drunk. Both stopped, unbuttoned trouser flies and pissed into the weeds Mrs Pearson called her garden.

'Did so get 'er in those bushes out the side,' Jake heard Gary yell at the top of his voice, clearly continuing with a conversation that had started as they had ridden home. 'She'd do anything for me, old Joyce would. She did, too.'

'Aw, yeah?' said Darcy. 'Only problem would be, you wouldn't know what to do back!'

'She got good fingers, Joyce.'

'Yeah, yeah, yeah.'

'Yeah,' and Gary started re-buttoning. 'Good feed, eh?'

'Get a move on. Need to go to bed. And don't talk about food,' said Darcy. 'Makes me feel like chucking up — again!'

Their voices lowered and Jake could hear nothing more of their conversation. He watched intently as they weaved a path into the house. He saw the light come on. He went on watching, wary, until the light went out. He stayed at his window for another ten, fifteen minutes before allowing the sacking curtain to flap back into place and then he crawled into his bed and slept for what was left of his night.

VII

They got him.

'Got 'im, Darce.' Gary was jubilant. One strong arm around the boy's neck and the other forcing Jake's arm up his back. 'Now what?'

'We tie the bugger up,' said Darcy. 'Here's the rope.'

'Only got two hands and I gotta use them to hold him,' said Gary, reasonably. 'I'm doin' me best. We don' want him to escape. That wouldn't be fair, eh?' Gary shook his head.

'I'll tie him, Gary,' said Darcy, patiently.

'Then can I punch 'im? Please, Darce, please let me punch him?'

'Sure. Reckon you've earned it,' Darcy grinned at his mate. 'But not too much and just for a little while. We don't want to knock him out. Got to make sure he's fully alive to enjoy the good bit. Wouldn't be fair if he's out of it.'

Jake struggled with every ounce of his strength. It was futile. Useless. Gary chuckled, thoroughly enjoying the struggles of his much smaller victim, controlling Jake with absolute ease.

In a small corner of his mind Jake realised, far too late, that he'd let down his guard too soon, grown unwary, maybe even thinking it had been nothing more than idle talk and that nothing worse than a bit of mean-spirited bullying, pushing, tripping, shoving would be his lot. He'd got through the milking, the cows had gone, the clean-up almost over and nothing had happened and they'd forgotten about him as they slept off their late night and too much beer.

How wrong he'd been. The looks on the faces of both his captors told him something far more vile than another round of idle bullying was about to take place. He started to tremble and this served to increase the enjoyment of the one who held him. 'Think he's gonna piss hisself,' giggled Gary. 'Looks like it. That'd be good, eh? Ya dirty little bugger.' He forced Jake's arm further up his back and shook him. 'You piss on me, you'll be sorry,' he hissed in Jake's ear. The stench of stale beer and cigarette smoke added to Jake's feeling of nausea.

Darcy said nothing, busied himself and quickly and efficiently had Jake tied, spread-eagled against the framework of one of the milking bays. There could be no escape. No way out.

Darcy and Gary stood back to enjoy the sight of their handiwork and have a smoke, lounging casually and congratulating each other on the results so far.

'Geez, I feel good now,' said Gary. 'Fresh air's got rid of me hangover.' He lit himself another cigarette.

'Oh, you'll be feeling even better soon,' said Darcy. 'He won't be,' he nodded at Jake.

Gary laughed happily. 'Good one, Darce. He sure as hell won't be feelin' better.' He laughed some more. 'You gotta good sense of humour. Now what?'

'I think now's your time for a bit of a punch up while I go and drag in his girlfriend,' said Darcy.

'His girl . . . Oh, yeah. I geddit. Great,' said Gary. 'Take ya time. I'll just punch him sorta soft and gentle. Like you said, we don' wanna knock him out. Not yet. I'll be very, very careful, I promise.

But I don' have to be too gentle, do I?'

'You just have a good time, mate. I'll only be a couple of minutes,' said Darcy.

Jake shut his eyes and clamped fast his mouth and waited for blows to fall. God help him but he wouldn't give this swine the satisfaction of hearing him call out.

Gary thoroughly enjoyed the light exercise provided by a well-trussed up and live punching bag and experimented with several good moves he'd observed in the one live boxing contest he'd attended. It was certainly good to have an opponent who was completely unable to return a blow or put up any sort of a fight. Much safer, that way. A pity, though, that his mate wasn't there to observe these fine moves of his. Great exercise, but not all that exciting without an audience! 'Geez, you're a dumb bugger,' was all he said to Jake. 'You just wait till Darce gets back. He's sure gotta good surprise for you. I'll have me another smoke. Bet you need one.' He grinned.

There wasn't long to wait.

'Bugger didn't want to come,' announced Darcy, returning. 'Wonder why?' he laughed. 'Had to be a bit nice to it, seeing as we want the sod to do its job. Come on, sucker,' he urged, and then he laughed. 'And that's just what it's going to be. Geddit? Sucker?'

'Nah. Don' think so,' said Gary, the fog of his mind as dense as his cloud of cigarette smoke. 'Oh, yeah. See what ya mean. I think.'

With unaccustomed care and gentle urging, Darcy Pearson steered a new-born bull calf towards Jake.

'Geez, you're sure bein' nice to it,' said Gary.

'Yeah. But not for too long. It's all yours to kill after it's done its work.'

A wide grin spread across Gary's face. 'Your dad won't mind?'

'Hell no. He gave it to me. Was due to go out the gate. Told Dad I wanted it for its skin for my room. You know. Another floor mat like the two I already got. It's all mine to do what I like with,' and Darcy tenderly stroked his prey.

'Yeah. You can do what you like with it, if it's yours. Fair enough, eh?' said Gary 'No one can say nuthin'. I'd like a calf floor mat for my room at home. Any chance of you giving me this bugger?'

Darcy looked at the calf. 'Don't see why not. It's nothing special. It can be your Christmas present,' he smiled.

'Thanks, Darce. I'll make sure I torture it gentle so's I don' hurt his nice skin. Sure gonna be nice'n soft on me toes on cold mornings,' said Gary. 'He's quite a fluffy bugger, eh? Must be his little baby furs.'

Jake was frozen still. Tied still. His mind couldn't grasp what possible horrors there could be that would involve both himself and the bewildered calf. The fate of the calf was as clear as day.

'I've starved it for just about two days,' Darcy smiled. 'It sure as hell needs a good feed,' and he stuck out two fingers of one hand and the hungry calf took them, sucked avidly.

Gary giggled. 'Stupid sod thinks you got milk in them fingers. No milk there, sucker.'

'No' said Darcy, laughing. 'But I reckon I know where there's some. Pull the bloody pongo's pants down.'

Gary was suddenly reluctant. 'Dunno if I wanna do that.'

'Then get in there and bring out one of the jugs of house milk,' Darcy nodded towards the milking shed. 'Might need a bit to use as bait. I'll do his pants,' and he advanced on Jake. 'Reckon you're not going to enjoy this one little bit, Pongo. Ooohh, it's going to hurt bad. Real bad.' He knelt, tore open the fly of the old trousers Jake was wearing and pulled them, and the boy's underpants, down around his ankles. He whistled tunelessly as he worked. 'Come on, Gary. Where the hell are you? Didn't tell you to milk a bloody cow.'

'Good stuff,' said Gary, smacking his lips and wiping away whiskers of milk. 'Just had a swig. Here.'

'Right,' Darcy took the jug. 'Grab that sodding calf and bring it here.' He sloshed the contents of the milk jug over Jake's private parts. 'Come on, calf. Suck!' he ordered. 'Pongo's only got one tit but it'll have to do and it's the last one you'll ever get.' He nudged the calf's nose and mouth to Jake's penis.

The hungry calf suckled.

Jake strained, writhed and began to moan, groaning both at the agony of the sandpaper-like suck and the humiliation that was being forced upon him. He made no effort now to hold back on the tears that rolled down his face. The pain intensified as the bull calf fought harder in an unavailing attempt to satisfy its hunger and thirst. It seemed that he stung and stung and stung more as his penis was rubbed, sucked raw against the roughness of the baby creature's rasping tongue.

The pleasure of the two torturers knew no bounds. They whooped, hollered and yelled with great glee at the marvellous effects of their actions. They slapped their thighs, they slapped each other's backs. 'Shit a brick!' exclaimed Darcy. 'Knew this'd be good when I heard about it. Boy, oh boy! Even better than I expected!'

'It's ya best one yet,' Gary agreed. 'And we can see it all. Oh, it's just so funny. Get stuck in there, calf. Can I boot it?'

'Sure you can,' said his mate, rolling around laughing. 'Do what you like now. Give it hell. Better drag it off, anyway. Better leave the pongo with something to piss with or I might be in trouble.' He joined his friend in a combination of rugby football, wrestling and boxing with the bellowing calf. Darcy untied one of Jake's arms. 'You can get yourself out of the rest of it, Pongo. And pull up your bloody pants. You look disgusting. No decent bloke wants to look at what you've got down there,' he chuckled. 'Or rather what's left of it.'

'Can I slit his throat now?' asked Gary.

'Of course you can. Pity we can't do the same to the pongo.' Still laughing, the two of them dragged the luckless calf to its fate.

Jake was left alone. Finally, he managed to untie himself. He looked at where he hurt the most and felt no more than a small sense of relief at the discovery that he was still intact. He hurt badly; in his mind as well as body. He didn't trouble to staunch his flow of tears as he stumbled, half blindly, back towards his hut.

Jake no longer cared what might happen to him if he left this place. He wasn't going to stay. Surely nowhere else could be anywhere near as bad as this place — not even prison.

He would leave.

There was a barrel of rainwater collected from the roof at the corner of his room. He washed himself, wincing at the sting of the cold water on his rubbed-raw penis. He dressed, putting on the clothes that were his own and which he had worn when he had first arrived at the farm. He packed his small cardboard suitcase. He found Little Black Sambo under the rotten floorboards and shoved the kitten into the pocket of his jacket.

Giving the farmhouse a wide berth, he took a farm track through the herd of mildly curious cows to where he knew track and roadway met. He came out onto the road and walked away, hobbling, crippled by the knife-sharp and red-hot pain in his groin.

VIII

It became harder to walk. The rawness between his legs wasn't helped by the rubbing of his clothing. Two, maybe three miles from the farm he stopped, left the gravel road and took shelter in a scrubby belt of macrocarpa trees. Jake was tired. The fitful, wary sleep of the night before, the early start on the cows, the milking — and then the agony of what had followed had hardly prepared him for a hike in the hot sun of early summer. He hid himself away and rested. He hadn't intended to sleep but exhaustion overcame him and he curled up in the shade of the trees and, at first, dozed. He unbuttoned the fly of his trousers, pulled clear his underpants and examined the damage. He was so sore. However, and he was aware of feeling a sense of relief, he appeared to still be all there! He cupped his private parts in his two hands in order to afford himself a little relief. Curling himself into a ball, still holding himself, he fell into a disturbed and haunted half sleep.

Mid to late afternoon he was woken by his kitten. Bored by the inactivity of his companion, and quite likely somewhat hungry, Little Black Sambo began an exploration of Jake's hair, head and face. The feel of another sandpaper tongue quickly woke Jake.

At first he couldn't work out where he was, what he was doing in this scrubby place. The heat of the day had gone and clouds scudded across the sky. Jake shivered slightly. Still sore, tired, and now very hungry, he sat up, leaned against a tree and thought about what to do. None of his options were particularly comforting.

First things first. He opened up his suitcase and ferreted in the jumbled contents, found what he was looking for. A couple of crusts of very dry bread, the left-overs from his theft of a couple of days before. He munched into one crust and put the other back in his case. The kitten sniffed at the crumbs it was being offered, at first ignoring them and then, as hungry as his master, tucked into them.

Below the bank of trees was a small stream, a run-off from a culvert under the road. The water looked clear, clean enough and he scooped sufficient into his mouth to satisfy his thirst. Jake sat back under the trees and thought about what to do.

His prospects appeared absolutely bleak and his options almost non-existent. Go back to the farm? No. Not that. There must be something else, somewhere else. But how to find it? He had no money. Not a penny. Well, he did have less than penny. In the top pocket of his Harris tweed jacket he had the one coin he could call his own — his 'good-luck farthing' as he called it, the tiny coin he'd picked up, wharf-side, on the day he and his sister, Janice, set sail from Liverpool. It seemed so long ago. One good-luck farthing wasn't likely to be able to provide for very much of a future. A quarter of a penny, the full extent of his fortune. A quarter of one penny and one more crust of dry bread!

'Might as well just get on and see what happens,' he said to his cat. 'Come on.' He tucked Little Black Sambo back into his jacket pocket, hobbled stiffly to his case, picked it up and walked on. He had no idea where this road might take him. He couldn't tell if it was indeed the same road he'd travelled on that wet night he'd arrived in this place. It didn't matter. It went somewhere. Somewhere well away from where he'd been.

The cat got tired of being imprisoned in a jacket pocket, escaped, and trotted along behind the boy. 'Well, if you get lost, Sambo, I can't say as I care. Not really,' said Jake. 'I think you could settle down anywhere round here and find a mouse or a rat or a bird or something. Just you remember, don't go back to that place. Your life wouldn't be worth living. Let any of 'em get their hands on you, you wouldn't have a life to live, anyway! Specially him!' He stumbled on. In time to his walking he began to chant, 'I will not back! I will not go back! I will not go back! I will not go back!' until his kitten stopped, sore of paw, mewing plaintively. Jake turned back to the animal, bent down, picked him up and shoved him into the pocket of his jacket. 'And now shut up or I'll leave you,' and he gently patted the pocket. Little Black Sambo did as he was told. 'I will not go back! I will not go back!'

But he was wrong.

There was no traffic on this back-country, unsealed road, but eventually the unsealed road ran out onto a sealed and secondary route that lead . . . well, Jake didn't know where. And now the occasional farm truck, the odd car. A few farmhouses. Maybe one house every quarter-mile or so. First, at the sound of an approaching vehicle, Jake took cover, dropping into ditches, behind a tree, and, once, awkwardly, painfully, climbing a fence into a paddock and dropping down to hide in some sort of crop.

It was coming on dark when, finally, he let his guard down. If a car or truck should spot him now and stop he would ask them to give him a ride to the nearest town. By now, he reasoned, he was far enough away from that hellhole so that anyone stopping wouldn't be able or even interested in making any sort of connection. He was sore, so sore. Maybe, even, he could make it through the night in some ditch or tree hideaway. Better by far, though, if he could make it to a town. He felt sure it would be better in towns. Not that spending a night in the country held any terrors for him. Gran's old cottage on the outskirts of a Hereford village might not have been the bare and empty countryside he was used to now but it had been, after all, country enough. He knew dark nights with no streetlights or traffic sound.

The vehicle, a car, slowed, stopped. The car window was rolled down. 'Well, then, me young rooster, where might you be off to at this time of night, suitcase and all? And what's that you got, a damned cat?' A man, middle-aged, alone in the car. Gruff.

'Can you give me a ride to town, please?' asked Jake.

'To town, you say?' Not unfriendly.

'Yes please.'

'And what town might that be?' A head came through the window and a face peered more closely at the boy.

'It doesn't matter,' said Jake, more alert, and he began to move on.

'Hang on a minute, boy. You come back here.' There was now a rough order in the tone of his voice.

'It doesn't matter,' repeated Jake, more alert still. He walked on. The car, quietly, engine purring, rolled towards him and again pulled up.

'Of course it matters,' said the man, less roughly. 'Can't have a kid of your age wandering God knows where about the country at this time of night. What would folks think?''

'I'm all right, sir. Thank you,' said Jake, very politely. Drive on, why don't you!

'Come on. Hop in. I'll take you to town. Come on now. Looks as if you could do with a lift.'

Jake sighed. He gave in. He was tired, very tired, sore. He walked around the car and opened the passenger-side door, stepped up and into the vehicle. The man held out a hand, took Jake's suitcase and tossed it over onto the back seat. 'Thank you,' said the boy.

'And where might you be from?' asked the man. The car started forward.

'Oh, I'm from round here,' said Jake.

'With an accent like that? Not likely, lad. I don't think so.' The car slowed, turned into a gateway, stopped, reversed out and headed back along the road in the direction Jake had come.

'Where are we going?' asked Jake. Sudden alarm.

The driver turned to him. He was now grinning broadly. Not a particularly friendly grin. 'Reckon I've copped myself a runaway. Only kid in the whole of these parts speaks like you do would be the farm lad out on the Pearson place that old Clarrie moans about to anyone who'll listen. Right?' He didn't wait for an answer. 'And don't you be trying anything stupid, lad. I'm the police round here. Day off and they still got me working,' he sighed. 'You running away? From a damn good home and a job? Humph! That's gratitude for you.'

Jake said nothing. Now he was terrified.

The man chuckled. 'Wonder what old Clarrie and his missus'll think of this little lot. Their bloody worker takin' off the minute their backs are turned,' he laughed. 'And stealing one of their farm cats! Wonder what else you've got in that bag of yours, eh?' he looked at Jake again. 'What's the matter, boy? Cat got your tongue?' and he laughed very loudly. 'Good folks, the Pearsons. Salt of the earth. And that boy of theirs? Fine young feller. Whatsisname? Good little forward. Asset to the club. Lot you could learn from him, boy.'

Jake said nothing. There was little time for conversation. The distance that had taken him half a day or more to cover had been eaten up by the policeman and his car in no more than a few minutes. The car turned into the Pearson drive, honked its horn very loudly and came to a stop at the Pearson backdoor. 'Here,' said the cop. 'I'll take your cat. You grab your bag,' and he picked up Little Black Sambo by the scruff of his neck and got out of the car.

'Look what I got here for you, folks,' he nodded at Jake. 'Reckon it belongs to you. Takin' off on a holiday, it seems. Cat and all!' he said to Mr and Mrs Pearson and Darcy who had come from the house to form a welcoming committee on the back doorstep. 'Ouch! Little devil scratched me. Where the hell's it gone?' and the constable sucked a scratched finger. Little Black Sambo hadn't stayed to join the gathering and had taken off into the night.

'Don't you worry, Mr Stannard,' said Darcy. 'I'll knock it on the head when I get my hands on it.'

'Good lad,' said the policeman.

There was grim silence around the kitchen table. Four pairs of eyes followed the policeman's every movement as he fossicked through the meagre contents of Jake's suitcase, tossing the bits and pieces of clothing to the floor after checking pockets and linings. The sole piece of stolen property was a crust of dry bread. Disappointment showed in three of the four pairs of eyes. 'Not to say the little wretch hasn't stashed a haul of your stuff between here and where I got him,' said the cop. 'If I were you folks I'd be doing a thorough check of your valuables.'

'Don't worry yourself, George. We will be,' Mrs Pearson, tight-lipped. 'We most certainly will be.' She turned to Jake who stood, head lowered. 'And this is all the thanks we get for providing you with a good home, a good job and three square meals a day out of the goodness of our hearts. God knows!' The woman was furious. 'Turn our backs for five minutes and you've scarpered, you ungrateful little beast . . .'

Jake spoke. He looked straight at her. 'He,' and he pointed to Darcy Pearson. 'He and his friend Gary tied me up and got a poor calf to suck my cock and then they killed it,' he raised his voice. 'You want to see what it did?' and his hands moved to his trouser fly.

'You disgusting little wretch,' the woman yelled. 'You . . . Words fail me!'

'Don't you listen to him, Mum. If you ask me, he's done it to himself. Bet he plays with himself all the time. He's done it to himself, all right. You ask Gary.'

'Shut up,' said his mother, turning on him.

Constable Stannard moved to Mrs Pearson and patted her shoulder. 'Don't you worry, Missus. I'm sure your good man, here,' and he nodded at Clarrie Pearson, 'I'm sure he'll have everything back in order in no time flat and will have sorted out this little lot.'

Mrs Pearson would not be placated. 'Idle little good-for-nothing . . . Get home here and the darn cows bellowing their heads off for milking and not a soul in sight and next to dark . . .'

'I was here, Mum,' Darcy said plaintively. 'I was just about to start the milking when I found he'd bolted.'

'Be quiet,' his mother snarled at him. 'I blame you near as much as I blame him. Left you in charge and look what happens!'

The cop felt that his part in the drama had been fully played and began moving to the door. 'I'll just be saying goodnight, then, folks. Leave you, Clarrie, to take whatever action you think necessary.'

He clapped Pearson on the shoulder and lowered his voice slightly. 'If he were mine, I know what I'd be doing to the little blighter,' he winked. 'Wouldn't be sitting down for a week, ungrateful little sod.'

'You've got my word on that, George.' Clarrie Pearson saw the policeman out of the backdoor. 'Won't be sitting down for a bloody month!' and the two of them laughed.

'Good man,' said the policeman, taking his leave.

IX

'Grab him,' snarled Clarrie Pearson as the sound of the policeman's car faded down the driveway. 'Don't want him getting away again, slippery little devil. We'll take him out the back, down to his room. He's about to learn a lesson he won't forget for a long time. You stay here, Mum,' he said to his wife. 'No need to trouble yourself with this. Man's work. May as well take his rubbish,' and he picked up Jake's case. 'You got him, boy?'

'Sure have, Dad.'

'Well, come on then.'

Jake was frog-marched out of the house, down the path to his room. Clarrie Pearson led the way.

'You're in the shit now, Pongo. You've got no idea what my old man can do when his temper's up. Believe me, I do. Wow!' Darcy's excitement knew no bounds. A good weekend was about to become a great weekend.

Jake whimpered. He tried hard to control himself but to no avail.

'Right, you little pommie bastard. Pull down your bloody pants. Seems you're quick enough at doing it and fiddling round with yourself when Mum'n me aren't around. Dirty little bugger. Come on, get 'em down and get yourself across that bed!'

Dumbly, numbly, Jake did as he was bid. There wasn't the

61

slightest chance of escape. The man unbuckled his own belt, a considerable length of wide leather, and said, 'A lesson you've got to learn, boy, and just you remember this is going to hurt me more than it hurts you!'

Darcy Pearson couldn't control himself. He laughed at the top of his voice and said, 'No it bloody won't, Dad.'

'Shut up, or you'll get it, too!' yelled his father. 'You're not too big for me to deal with, and don't you forget it,' which swiftly silenced his son. 'Come on! Get across that bed! Get your arse-end on the edge, boy!' and he raised his belt.

The first blow brought an in-drawn breath from Jake. At first, the pain was nowhere near as intense as he had thought it would be. But then it started to spread, seeping down his legs, up his back.

'Good for you, Dad,' Darcy couldn't help but cheer his father on.

'I thought I told you to shut up!' yelled the enraged man, and raising his belt he brought it, whistling, down again — this time it lashed and curled around his son's legs.

Darcy yelped, jumped and screamed. 'Dad, no . . . no!'

'Then shut your mouth,' said his father, turning back to Jake.

In a tiny little corner of his mind Jake thought to himself that he no longer cared how many blows he had to take from this man, he'd experienced the satisfaction of seeing his chief enemy squealing in pain.

Jake took two more blows from Clarrie Pearson. He registered the pain, wincing, shrinking at the savagery of the wicked leather. He held his mind, however, clear on one joyful thing, the look of abject fear and terror on Darcy Pearson's face as he suffered his one lash.

The fourth blow. The belt raised. The red-faced and sweating

Pearson, straining to get the utmost force behind the blow took half a step back. His foot found one of the rotten boards and he lost balance. Arms flailing he toppled backwards, clutching, as he fell, at anything that might stop his fall. His hand caught at a jagged, rusting and very sharp edge of the corrugated iron wall. The skin of his palm tore, blood spurted. 'Jesus Christ!' he screamed. 'Bloody done for myself!' He righted himself to a crouch, his uninjured hand cradling his bleeding hand and fingers. Snarling like a wounded animal, he staggered to his feet. He turned to his son who stood, open-mouthed. 'Finish off the little swine,' he said as he lurched from the room.

Darcy Pearson required no second bidding. There was now a score to settle and he'd been invited to settle it. Jake had twisted, curling around and resting on one elbow, half on and half off his bed. White-faced and trembling, he made one feeble attempt to get to the door but didn't stand a chance. Darcy was there before him. One boot in Jake's chest forced him back onto his bed.

'And now it's just you and me,' Darcy muttered through gritted teeth, absolute venom in his voice, his eyes glittering. Almost negligently he took Jake by one arm, twisted it, flipping the smaller boy over onto his stomach with ease. Using the same hand he pulled Jake's pants down to his knees and then his shirt up to his neck. 'I hate you, you little pommie bastard,' he hissed. He reached for his father's belt that lay on the floor and finished the beating his father had started.

There was none of the older man's self-righteousness in Darcy Pearson's assault on Jake. There was also one other critical difference. Clarrie Pearson had held the belt by the buckle. His son reversed this order.

Jake screamed once, very loudly. He screamed a second time,

but it was more muffled. His small body convulsed at the savagery being inflicted upon it. Blessedly, he lost full consciousness. At some stage, after about ten or a dozen blows the dreadful enormity of his frenzied actions got through to Darcy Pearson. All of a sudden he saw what he had done. The criss-cross of lashes, bleeding, raw on the boy's back and buttocks . . . the stillness of his victim. He shut his eyes, opened them again. The sight hadn't gone away. 'Arrgh . . . ' was the only sound he made. Throwing the belt from him, he turned, rushed from the room and back to the house.

Some two hours later Jake came back into his senses. His body burned with a fiery intensity. Slowly he made himself sit. He felt around to his back, groaning at the pain. He withdrew his hand and looked at it, his eyes dull. It was covered in blood. He tried to stand. He swayed, groggy. He fell down again, back onto the bed.

The light was still on. He had no idea what time it was or how long he had lain in his own blood. He looked down. Not only in his own blood. In his own blood and piss.

He summoned every tiny atom of energy within his battered body and stood, forced himself to walk. Every step tore his aching body further apart. He walked a little more, up and down the room. It got easier. Slowly, with infinite care, he pulled off his shirt and pants. He shivered, from the after-shock of his battering as much as from the cool night air. From the jumble of his clothing that had been thrown into the room he picked out what he thought would be the most comfortable and, even more slowly now, dressed himself and put on what footwear he could find. He couldn't stop crying, didn't even know he was crying. Finally, he picked up his Harris tweed jacket and dragged himself from the room.

He crept and he crawled, did Jake. Along ditches, scraps of roadway, farm tracks, over or under fences, into trees and scrubby bush through swampland, farmlands, across streams. At some stage he came to the railway line and followed the track for a mile or so until he imagined he heard the approach of a train. Some instinct drove him onward and away from the Pearson farm. Sometimes he was within his mind, at other times he could have been anything, anywhere. He didn't really know what he did, but he covered ground, he made distance from the place of his agony.

As dawn broke exhaustion overcame him and he crawled into a cave of grasses and flax, took cover and slept. Sometime in the early afternoon he came to, bewildered, bemused, feverish. The pain he now felt ripped and burnt with a fierce and bright intensity, consuming his entire body. There were no more tears. He didn't have any spare energy for the luxury of tears.

Neither did he feel hunger. He took water when he could find it in ditches, streamlets and, once, from a puddle on a roadway. In the hours he poured into that incredible trek he saw not one other living soul. Some instinct kept him away from places of human habitation. There were times when he thought he might die, but some inner spark kept him going. Jake crawled on.

On a grassy embankment he stopped for a moment to regain a vestige of strength. At first he thought he was dreaming and he blinked through mucous encrusted eyes at what he saw. It was dusk, and what had taken his attention were the lights of a town.

Slowly, agonisingly, he dragged himself towards those lights. His shoes were gone, by some miracle he still had one sock, and the Harris tweed jacket was somewhere in the back of beyond. He had no thought other than that wherever he ended up, nothing could be as bad as what he'd left.

Towards midnight he reached the town. His journey had taken more than a day. Delirious now, he managed to stand and stagger into the outskirts. As he reached the first of those lights, they all went out. He stood, stock-still, for a moment and somewhere within a corner of his mind there registered a thought that he might have died. He shook his head, moved on. Of course he hadn't died. Death would mean release from the all-consuming pain.

Jake never knew he crossed two or three streets of the darkened town. Mercifully, his agony closed in upon him and he collapsed, passing completely from consciousness. His small, broken body fell into the resisting growth of a garden at the gateway of a large house.

1947-1948

I

'Didn't happen to collect the paper as you rode in, Molly?' the man asked.

'I wasn't looking,' said the woman. 'I'm normally not here at this time and you've usually had the paper hours before I get here. If it weren't for those dratted curtains . . .'

'All right, all right, woman. No need for a lecture. Have another cup of tea and I'll wander down.'

'No time for tea,' she said. 'Got to get those curtains down, washed and dried and up again. God knows, another day up there and they'll be falling from the weight of their own dirt.'

'Please yourself, there's plenty in the pot. Back in a minute,' and picking up a walking stick he went out into the early morning sun.

He couldn't find his newspaper and cursed the paper boy in a ritual and good-humoured curse he offered up most mornings. 'Little blighter does it on purpose! Where's he flung it this time?' He began his customary search in and around the border of hydrangeas at the front of the property. 'Not again!' he grumbled. 'Bloody dogs wrecking every damn thing I try to grow,' and he moved, limping slightly, towards one bush he could see was out of kilter with its neighbours. 'I don't believe it! Some little devil actually hiding in the damn thing!' He raised his voice. 'Out of there, you limb of Satan! What d'you think you're playing at?' and using his walking stick he poked at the form hiding in the bush. 'Out of there. Let's be having you!' There was no reaction. None at all. With some difficulty, the man knelt.

'Sweet Mother of Jesus!' He cast both stick and his afflictions aside and crawled to the body, breaking away the soft growth of the plant. He said nothing more for a moment. With well-practised ease he felt the forehead, raised a closed eyelid, lifted a wrist, felt for a pulse. 'Dear Christ. What in God's good name has befallen you?' He got to his feet, looked around, saw nothing else, and as fast as a gammy leg would allow, made his way back up the driveway, yelling, 'Molly! Woman! Molly! Molly, where are you?'

'What is it now?' She came out of the front door. 'What's . . .'

'Come on, woman. Stretcher. I'll need your help. There's that old stretcher in the surgery the St John's folk borrow . . . Child, down there at the gate . . . badly injured. We'll get him back to the surgery.'

'You can't lift . . .'

'Don't tell me what I can and can't do! I'll . . . We'll do it.'

With speed and with infinite care, the old doctor, his housekeeper and Robert, the late-arriving newspaper boy, moved Jake from his bed of hydrangea, onto the stretcher, up the driveway, through the house and into the surgery. 'Well done,' the doctor nodded to the other two. 'As for you, you grinning imp of mischief, now I've got you at my mercy, throw my damn paper in the driveway in future.'

'Yes, Dr Mac.'

'Get down there and find my stick and bring it back and put my paper on the kitchen table and then get the hell out of here or you'll be late for school.' All the while he continued tending to Jake.

'Gee, Dr Mac, can't I stay and watch? Reckon he'll die?'

'Out! Out!' was the only reply and his helper left.

Molly Henderson stood at Jake's head, stroked his matted hair. 'Who? What?' she looked at the doctor. 'Mac, even I can see someone has done this to him.'

'That's as may be. If you're going to stay, woman, make yourself useful.' He handed her scissors. 'Start cutting off his clothing. All of it. No need to be too gentle, he's well out to it and will be even more so with this in him.' He injected Jake and they worked on in silence until, together, they turned Jake to lie on his stomach and Molly Henderson peeled away the last of the clothing that covered the boy's back.

'And I thought I'd seen everything,' said the doctor, very softly.

'He's so . . . he's so thin. Little mite,' said Molly Henderson. 'Are you all right?' She looked at her employer. 'Pain? Your fingers?'

'No more than usual. Fingers still know what they have to do.' He looked down. 'Any pain I have is nothing compared with what this little feller has felt.'

'What else can I do?' asked Molly.

'You've done enough. Barbara will be here by ten. I'll sing out if I need more help.'

'Make sure you do. I'll bring you in a cuppa. Shall I ring through to the hospital? The ambulance?'

'No,' said the doctor, and stretched the sound of the word. 'Not just yet.'

'The police?'

'The police?' He looked again at Jake. He spoke slowly. 'I suppose . . . No. I think we'll wait just a little while . . .'

'Are you sure, Mac?' She sounded worried.

'On my head be it,' said the doctor. 'I think I'll wait until the boy comes round. He'll get no better attention from cop or hospital than he's getting here. No broken bones that I can tell. Bit too soon to

70

tell about a broken spirit,' he looked at his housekeeper. 'I'll call if I need help, but I think I can bend and twist enough life out of these old fingers to do a bit of embroidery. A goodly number of stitches needed on the reverse side of this little monkey.'

'Poor boy,' she said. 'I wonder who he is? Someone must be missing him.'

He spoke slowly. 'Not a town kiddie, Molly. Between the two of us we'd surely know that. Not a local . . . not quite. Country laddie? Don't know. Some bell's ringing in the back of my mind . . . ' he turned to her. 'Take a good, hard look, Molly, at the damage that's been done to the child. A good look. Remember it, your memory may be needed. There's one more thing you can do.'

'What's that?'

'Bring me my camera. The good one. It's through in the study, I think. Forget the curtains, woman. They'll hang for another year — or maybe it's time for some new ones. If you can spare a moment, check that the little bedroom just along the hall is shipshape.' He looked down at Jake. 'Very old, very soft sheets. Old ones.'

'The sheets are all old,' said Molly. 'Overdue for some new ones in that department, too! I'll price some for you when I pick up the curtain samples.' She winked at him as she left the surgery and the doctor settled to work.

His practice nurse, Barbara Green, arrived before ten. 'What on earth do you think you're doing? It's all right. Molly's told me. Here. Give it to me. Doctors!' she sniffed. 'Think you know it all. I'll fix up your stitching.'

'It's as perfect a bit of work you'll see this side of the black stump,' he said.

'Tell that to the marines!' she said. 'We've got a bit of work to do here.'

'I'd almost finished, when you so rudely interrupted me,' said the doctor.

'You know that's not what I meant,' she said. The two of them spoke with the familiarity of working partners who'd been in business for a long time.

'How many down for this morning?'

'Only old lady Stacy — and don't worry, Molly's already phoned her and she'll come this afternoon.' She examined Jake. 'You've done a passable job, Mac,' she smiled. 'He'll be coming round any time now. And what's all this nonsense about Molly making up a bed? Why?'

'I don't know why. Humour an old man. No more, maybe, than I looked at this poor little laddie and thought that the last thing he needed right now was Matron Lil up at the hospital, good woman that she is, regimenting him at six in the morning, breathing hellfire and brimstone and acting the sergeant-major.'

Barbara Green laughed. 'I'll tell her you said that!'

'No you won't. Besides, the place is full. He'd have to be trucked off down to the city.'

'You can't have him here, Mac. You don't even know who he is.'

'Not a hundred percent sure, but I think I do, Babs. Come on. We'll get him through to his bed and we'll talk in there. He's stirring himself up from whatever dark nightmare he's been through. Come on, little lad, let's get you through to a proper bed.' He sighed. 'Then I guess I'd better get to work on the telephone.'

Jake came to in a little blue bedroom. Three old faces looked down. As they loomed in and out of focus, he flinched and despite the pain, pulled himself away, cowering into the furthest corner of the bed.

'It's all right, boy. It's all right. You're safe. Do you understand?' James McGregor spoke slowly, loudly.

Jake didn't speak. He couldn't speak. A slight groaning sound was all he made.

'Don't speak, child,' said Barbara Green. 'Just give a little nod if you understand. You are safe. Just nod if you understand.'

His eyes, pain-filled, grogged, closed again. But he did nod before slipping again from consciousness.

'Hospital,' said Barbara Green, very firmly.

'No,' said the doctor. 'He's got a bad couple of days ahead of him but he's all in one piece. A ragged piece, admittedly, but he's all there. This old place has catered for more than a few damaged souls over the years.'

'Molly?' Barbara turned to the other woman for support.

'Strange as it may be, I find myself agreeing with Mac. God knows what the boy's been through but I have a feeling it's a bit of comforting he'll be needing rather than dear old Lil's camp on the hill. She's tops on broken limbs but not too hot on broken hearts and spirits.'

'Mac can't care for him,' said Barbara.

'Not by himself, he can't,' said Molly.

'Stop talking about me as if I weren't here. Been a quack for forty years. Wouldn't think that one battered kid would be beyond my fading capabilities.'

'Well it would be,' said Molly. 'Except, if he's to stay here, I shall move in for the next few days . . .'

'God help me,' said the doctor.

'No more than you deserve,' said his nurse. 'Don't worry,' she sighed. 'I'll lend a hand.'

James McGregor smiled. 'I knew you would! Both of you.' He looked at his nurse. 'Now to the nasty bit. Get on to the constabulary for me, Barbara. Not the local chappie. Never had much time for

73

him, and I've a hunch . . . Get me Bob Davis, the boss down the city. Old Bob owes me more than a few.'

'Who d'you think this boy is?' asked Barbara.

'I wouldn't be betting on it, not just yet,' James McGregor stroked Jake's head. 'But I've a feeling it's the little English laddie, war orphan or some such, came to live — and presumably work — on the Pearson property. You'd know the folks, both of you.'

'Of course we know them,' said Molly Henderson.

Jake stirred back into consciousness. 'He's trying to say something,' said Barbara. 'Don't worry, little lad. You're all right now. You just rest.'

'Let him speak,' said the doctor. 'Here . . . slip a few drops of this down his throat,' and he passed a feeding cup to the nurse. 'What is it you want to say, boy?' softly. 'Who are you lad? What's your name?'

They thought he said he was Jack. He said the one word three, four times, and then, before slipping away again he said something else another couple of times. 'Can't make it out,' said Molly Henderson. 'Something, I think, about a black sambo.'

'No. I don't think so. It's something about a cat. I'm sure,' said Barbara.

'Black Sambo, it's a kiddies' book,' said Molly. 'Yes. There he goes again.'

'Something and nothing,' said James McGregor. 'Let him rest now. I'll give him another jab.'

'Infection?' the nurse queried.

'Minimal so far,' said the doctor. 'There'll be some, but the scraggy little blighter should fight it off. I've pumped enough penicillin into him to bring a dead horse back from the grave. If, as I suspect, he's dragged himself all the way here, unaided, and over some rather tough terrain, he's a helluva lot stronger than he looks. Judging by the state of his hands and feet I doubt that anyone dumped him in my hydrangeas. Come on ladies, leave him be. Back to sleep with you, little Jack.'

Jake slept. Occasionally he would stir restlessly. Not often. Not even the noise of the house, the old doctor's surgery or a trail of patients crunching up the gravel drive and gossiping in the waiting-room next door disturbed him. From time to time James McGregor would come into the room and check on him.

The doctor phoned the police. 'Bit irregular, by-passing my local chap, Jim, but I'll take your word for it,' the inspector said. 'Your word's always been good enough for me. I'll make it in the morning and bring a couple of my boys with me. You think the lad will be up to talking?' And then, 'Twist Molly Henderson's arm, will you? I could go a round or two with her date scones.'

Early evening and Robert, the newspaper boy, cycled up the doctor's drive and knocked on the door.

'Yes? What d'you want?' asked the doctor.

'Come to see about that boy I rescued. Will he live?' asked Robert.

'Mind your own business,' said the doctor. 'Why aren't you at school.'

'It's six o'clock! They have to let us out sometimes, Dr Mac.'

'More's the pity. And what d'you mean, you rescued?'

'Couldn't have done it by yourself, not even with old Mrs H. givin' you a hand.'

'I heard that, Robert,' Mrs Henderson came out. 'That's enough of the *old*!'

'Sorry, Mrs Henderson,' said Robert.

'That's all right, Robert,' she smiled. 'I forgive you,' and she disappeared.

'And while you're here, uninvited and littering my doorstep, I have a bone to pick with you, you grinning layabout,' said the doctor.

'Look, Dr Mac, it's not my fault you got a jungle in your front garden,' Robert anticipated. 'I do my best. Mum says I have to do my best for you because you delivered me. The settlers spent about a hundred years knocking down the bush and here you are growing it all again. Don't blame me if you can never find your paper,' he grinned. 'Besides, look at it another way. Gives you a bit of exercise and that's supposed to be good. You should know, you're a doctor.'

'Exercise be damned,' said James McGregor. 'It's my bloody morning paper I need!

'How's the boy? Is he up the hospital? I'm not goin' up there to see him with old . . .'

'I'm not surprised. I bet you fire her paper in the right place! The boy is still here.'

'Was he too far gone to move up the hill? When's he gonna die? He was pretty bashed up, eh? I reckon someone done it to him.'

'He'll be all right, given a little time.' The doctor looked at his newspaper boy. 'Thank you for your help this morning, Robert. You're right. The old lady'n me, we couldn't have done it without your strong arms and legs. He's sleeping. Come on. You can check for yourself he's not dead.'

'Don't look too good to me,' said Robert, looking down on Jake. 'You sure he's not dead? Can I take his pulse? I know how.'

'No. Take my professional word for it, Robert. Now, then, off with you.'

II

At around midnight Molly Henderson tiptoed into Jake's room. The light was dim. James McGregor sat in a chair by Jake's bedside. He had fallen asleep, head back and lightly snoring and his glasses askew, over one ear and off the other. The morning newspaper lay spread on the floor. The woman smiled at something else; at some time or another the boy's badly cut and scratched hand had met up with that of the old doctor, almost a handshake grip.

She woke him gently. 'Come on, Jim, off to bed with you. I'll take over.' She looked at Jake. 'Poor little sausage hasn't the foggiest idea where he is, and if he wakes up I'll call you. I'll have an extra hour or so in the morning and you can get your own breakfast.'

'Yes,' said the doctor. 'He's resting easy enough now. The pain'll give him gyp when he does wake.' He looked up. 'Thank you, Molly. He muttered more about this kitten book, the Sambo one. Seems the only thing on his mind that surfaces.' The old man got to his feet.

'I don't know,' said Molly Henderson. 'If my memory serves me right, *Little Black Sambo* is definitely a kiddie's story about a little black feller in Africa.'

'Who knows,' said the doctor. 'Is there a cuppa out there?'

Daylight crept into the room soon after six in the morning. Jake woke. He lay absolutely still, as wary as ever. His body burned, pained, tortured. He turned his head one way and then the other. Where was he? How had he got here? And who was this old woman sitting asleep in a chair next to his bed? He turned slowly to get a closer look and the pain blasted through him. 'Shit!' he said, quite loudly.

Molly woke, started. 'Shhh . . . shhh . . .'

Jake's mouth worked and then in a hoarse croak he said. 'Sorry, missus.'

'Don't talk, love,' she said. 'Here, I'll get you something to whet your whistle. No, you just stay where you are, I'll see you get a few mouthfuls.' Gently, she supported his head and helped him to drink a little water.'

'Where am I?' he whispered.

She told him.

'I hurt all over.'

'I know, love. You just lie back now.'

Then he started up in the bed. The pain was excruciating and he screamed, his eyes started from their sockets and he reminded her again of a hunted and wounded animal. 'Th. . . th . . .they're not . . . here for me,' in a terrified stammer.

'Shhhh,' she soothed. 'There's no one here, love, except for me and the doctor — and here he is right now. No one here, luvey. No one at all. You're safe.'

He slumped back. 'I hurt,' and he looked up at both of them from helpless, pain-filled eyes.

'And I can do something about that, my friend. Might hurt just a bit more before it feels better but I've got a feeling you're man enough to take it. Let's be having a look at you now.'

'Don't you . . .' Jake held up a hand. 'Don't put me back to sleep. I don't want to be asleep when they come for me . . . No!' He coughed, exhausted by his effort.

'Listen, boy,' the old doctor spoke seriously, almost sternly. 'No one is coming for you that you don't want. Believe me,' he smiled. 'Trust me. Might just be one old lady and one old man — but no one'll be getting past either of us!'

For the first time in a very long time Jake smiled. A glimmer of a smile, but a smile for all that. 'I . . . believe you, sir,' he said.

'What's your name, lad?'

'Jacob John Neill.'

'Good name. Jacob John Neill, you say. Midlands?'

'Coventry.'

'Hmm. Should've picked it. Not been here long, have you? Been on a farm?'

He started to cry.

'It doesn't matter, boy.'

'Stop interrogating him, Jim,' said Molly Henderson. 'If you ask me, this young man is ready for a bit more sustenance than water and glucose. I'll just pop through and scramble him up an egg and maybe a little warmed milk. You do something to make him a bit more comfortable and leave your questions until later,' she ordered.

'Women,' said the doctor, winking at Jake. 'One day you'll learn it pays to do exactly what they tell you, Jacob John Neill. How old are you?'

'Nearly fifteen, sir.'

'Hell's bells, boy! She'd better do half a dozen eggs. Got to get a bit of padding on this frame of yours. You're almost a man!' For all his pain, Jake smiled broadly at James McGregor. 'Now, to wipe that grin off your face,' said the doctor. 'I've got to have a look at you. It'll hurt.'

'That's all right,' said Jake.

'Hah! No it's not. I mean, it will hurt. I've got to look at my stitching and cobbling of yesterday . . .'

'Was I here yesterday? What was I doing here yesterday?'

'Yes, you were here yesterday. We gathered up the wreckage of you from my front garden in the early hours of yesterday morning. You smashed a perfectly fine hydrangea, you destructive little devil. You'll pay for it!'

Jake grinned. 'I haven't got any money.'

'I'd take it out of your hide, that's if you had any left! Now turn over and get ready to hurt a bit. While I'm doing this I'm going to ask you some questions, just a few. I don't want you jumping out of the little bit of your skin that's left if I say something that brings up a bad memory. There is no one outside that door,' he pointed. 'No one out there who's going to take you anywhere you don't want to go.'

The doctor worked and questioned. Jake squeaked, squealed and answered as best he could. James McGregor hadn't lied. It hurt. 'Right, then, Jacob John Neill, turn back over. And now,' he uncovered the boy. 'Maybe you could tell me what's happened to this fellow down here,' he pointed at Jake's penis.

For a moment Jake was silent and he trembled. He looked at the man. 'Do I have to . . .' The old doctor nodded. Jake's lip trembled. He looked down at himself, looked at the doctor again and then told him what had happened.

James McGregor turned from the boy's bed for a moment, his eyes closed. He turned back to Jake and smiled, 'Never you mind, boy. You're still all there and it will heal quicker than you think. Try and eat a little something of what Mrs Henderson has cooked and then I'll rub in a few salves and potions and fill you with a few pills for this and that. Now then, I hear old Molly trudging this way. Just one last thing . . . later this morning the police will be here . . .'

80

There was an indrawn breath from Jake, a scream and a flinching away as if he had been struck. 'Nooooo . . .' One long drawn out cry.

'Stop it, boy!' the doctor was loud and very firm. 'It will not be, I repeat, not be the constable you tell me took you back to the farm. Do you understand?'

Jake blinked a couple of times and began to relax. 'I . . . I understand. They won't take me . . .'

'No, Jacob. No one will be taking you anywhere for some long time, and most definitely not until you've healed. And now, my fine young fellow, force as much of this fine fare down that gullet of yours as it will take. We've got to get you back on your feet before you wear out your backside!'

Jake grinned again. 'Is it all right if I ask something?'

'Fire ahead.'

'What's your name?'

'James McGregor. Doctor of this parish.'

'Are you Mrs McGregor?' he asked Molly.

'No, lad,' she laughed. 'There are some things not even I'm game for!'

'Where am I?' he asked.

'In the doctor's house,' said Molly Henderson.

'No, I don't mean that. I mean, what place is this?'

'Of course,' and she smiled. 'Weatherley. Nice enough little spot. Now, then, you get that egg down you — or as much as you can manage.'

There were three policemen. Two old ones and a young one. Inspector, sergeant and constable. The doctor ushered them into

Jake's room. The boy was dozing but his rest was fitful, painful, and he was alert, on-guard within seconds.

'Inspector Davis, this is Jacob John Neill, although I think he likes to be called Jake,' said the doctor. 'Jake, these gentlemen have a few questions for you. They already know a little bit from me but they have to hear of your er . . . adventures, from your own mouth. Right?'

'Yes,' whispered Jake.'

'Now then, boy,' the inspector began. 'What've we got here? Just tell me in your own words everything that's happened. The good doctor here tells me you're in a bit of a mess. Seems to me you must have some sort of guardian angel,' he smiled at Jake. 'Ending up as you did in his pride and joy — his front garden! Did you know where you were? No, don't bother answering that. Start from the beginning, don't leave anything out and don't worry if you see these two fellows taking notes.'

Jake told his story. Hesitant, stumbling, sometimes stammering . . . and then, when he saw there was nothing to fear, his confidence grew.

His audience listened attentively. Occasionally Bob Davis would ask the boy to repeat a fragment. Sometimes he would question. The sergeant and constable wrote plentiful notes.

Jake's story ended with the thrashing he had received at the hands of the Pearsons, father and son. No amount of prompting could winkle from him what he had endured or, indeed, how he had achieved the feat of getting from the Pearson farm to this bed in the home of Dr James McGregor. Jake's memory of his trek was well-clouded.

'Right, then,' said the inspector. 'That will do for going on with,' he beckoned to his team. 'One or two things before we leave here,' and he gave a series of orders. 'And now, Jim, we'll polish off a few of your Molly's fine scones and then be on our way. Maybe you could spare Molly to come out to the farm with us, Jim? She can sort the boy's belongings, his bits and pieces. He won't be going back there,' he spoke firmly.

'We'll leave you for a while, lad,' said James McGregor. 'Get some rest. I'll check up, or Nurse Green will, between our paying customers for the morning. OK?' he looked down, and then remembered. 'Just one little thing. This Sambo you've been gabbling on about in your sleep . . . book of yours, is it? Seems to have been a treasure of some sort. I'll have Mrs Henderson check on it for you when she goes out there.'

Jake blinked, as if uncomprehending. He looked into the faces of the three police, and most particularly at that of the young constable, a broad and pleasant face that smiled at him very slightly. The boy shivered, almost imperceptibly, and then said, 'Don' . . . don' . . . don't know what it could . . . must've been just a bad dream, I think.'

III

The day passed and Jake went on sleeping. They checked on him, doctor and nurse, from time to time, but otherwise left him alone. It was late afternoon when he stirred, woken by the noise of people arriving at the house. This time there was little wariness in his waking. Jake was beginning to feel safer.

Doctor and police inspector came into his room. 'I'll not trouble you much more just now, boy. I thought you would like to know what has happened. We've made three arrests — you understand what that means?'

Jake nodded.

'Mr Pearson, his son, Darcy, and the son's friend Gary Miller, the mechanic boy, all will face charges. One of the three, the son, faces very serious charges. They're on their way now, down to the city, along with my sergeant and the local chappie who'll be staying down there for the time being. Young Jackson, who was here with me this morning, will take over up here temporarily. He'll be in to see you later. I'm picking the magistrate or justices will make sure the Pearson lad will be held in custody. It's likely the other two will be given bail. Now, lad, bail is when . . .'

'I know what bail means, sir,' said Jake.

'So there, Bob,' said the doctor, smiling.

'Bright customer you've got here, Jim,' said the cop, winking.

'Just one more thing, boy. Now, don't you worry, it is beyond the realm of possibility that any responsible authority would return you to that farm. Understand?'

'Yes.'

'There is one painful thing I'm going to ask you.'

'Yes?'

'I've got Mrs Pearson out in the car. I think it is important that she sees for herself the damage that's been done to you by her menfolk. Are you feeling up to it?'

'You . . . you mean, see her?'

The policeman nodded. 'Yes. Just for a moment or two. Nothing to worry about. I'll be here, and I shall ask Mrs Henderson to be in here, too. Another woman, you know.'

'This way, Eunice. Through here,' he heard Molly Henderson.

Jake looked straight ahead. His heart pounded. It pounded right up into his throat and he thought it would jump from his body. He knew she was there but he wouldn't look at her and was thankful when James McGregor indicated for him to lie on his stomach. Thankful, too, for the pain that came with the removal of bandage and dressing. The pain distracted.

She said nothing. Stony-faced and still. And then, as the doctor stood aside and indicated the damage, there was one long in-drawn breath, a gasp. Jake heard her being taken from his room. She hadn't spoken to him and he hadn't spoken to her. He heard her say, 'Are you positive he couldn't have done it to himself?'

'Only if he were a professional contortionist, madam!' the inspector barked. 'Even then I suggest you ask yourself why anyone would want to do something like that to themselves!'

Jake thought she had gone and slowly turned over. She was in the doorway, looking straight at him. She looked different from how

85

he had ever seen her look before. Her mouth was open. He could see she had been crying. 'My boy,' she said, to no one in particular, 'My Darcy is a good boy. He is . . . he wouldn't have . . . couldn't have . . .' She didn't finish.

He'd never seen a bathroom like it before. Not in all his born days. It was just about a house in itself — the Buckingham Palace of bathrooms! For all his pains and discomforts he explored every corner. Two bowls for washing your face and a bath big enough to swim in — except he couldn't swim. He could learn to swim in this one!

'Everything all right, love,' Mrs Henderson knocked, called out.

'Yes. Yes thank you,' and, hastily, 'but could you please tell me where the lavatory is? Is it outside?'

'No, love. Try the other door. The cream one. Do you need a hand?'

'No,' very quick.

He pissed. He had held it back as long as he could, not trusting what might come. He knew he'd wet in his bed, but at least that had been while he slept. It wasn't as sore this time and Jake breathed a long and satisfied sigh of enormous relief. The sticky brown ointment applied by the old doctor was working its magic. Back in the bathroom he examined himself in the mirror. The reflection that looked back wasn't reassuring. The tousled head of fair hair was matted, hard to the touch. The scratches on his face were livid, and made more so by whatever it was the doctor had rubbed into the broken skin. One of his ears had been torn and he could see James McGregor's stitching and a band of painting in some orange-red stuff that extended over and down one cheek. And his eyes? It was a bit hard to see whether he had any.

'I'm coming in, anyway, young man. Let's be having you then!'

Molly opened the door. 'Come on. Let's be having you.'

He held up a hand to hide a giggle. 'That's what my mum always used to say.'

'Did she, dear?' the woman smiled, and she saw quickly that he'd been examining himself. 'Not quite a feast for sore eyes! Your mum say that, too?'

'I think so,' he said.

'Don't worry, young man. We'll soon have you polished up and fit to put on a postcard, you mark my words. It's mostly surface. And I'll just bet your mum also used to tell you beauty is only skin deep.'

'And ugliness goes right to the bone,' said Jake. 'I'd like to brush my hair.'

'I'll do it for you,' Molly Henderson smiled. 'Then it's back to your bed and I'm poaching us a nice bit of fish for our dinners and I'm sure if you're fit enough to be admiring yourself in a mirror, you'll be up to tucking into that. Come on, now. That nice young policeman's here to see you.'

'No more questions, Jake. Reckon the old bloke asked you more'n enough for one day and it's another day tomorrow,' Constable Barry Jackson grinned down at Jake. 'Didn't trust me, did you?'

'I don't know what you mean, sir.'

'Don't need to call me sir. I've got something for you.' He bent down, reached just out of the doorway behind him and held up a sugar sack.

The sack squirmed and gave out a muffled, 'Miaow.'

'Reckon this chap is your Little Black Sambo,' and he smiled again. 'Not all of us around here knock off every little animal we come across, although, to be honest I must admit I felt a bit murderous about

Little-Black-Devil-From-Hell. Claws sharp as needles.' The constable smiled as Jake struggled to undo the cord knotted around the sack.

'He's still alive,' he marvelled. 'He survived!'

'Surely did,' said the cop, ruefully. 'I'm carrying the proof of that!'

Little Black Sambo lay in the bottom of the sack looking balefully up at his owner. He added a further scratch or two to Jake's hand and wrist before curling up in the crook of his arm and going to sleep.

'One helluva kitten,' said Barry Jackson. 'Now, I've got to go. Got to telephone my girlfriend. She's going to murder me, stuck up here in the sticks for the next month.'

'Thank you,' said Jake.

'I didn't know what you were thinking about this morning when you gave me that look, kid, but you've got no need to worry about me. Trust me?'

'I do now,' said Jake. 'Sir,' he added.

'No, Robert. You can't see him,' said Mrs Henderson. 'We're about to eat.'

'I'll wait,' said Robert. 'Unless you're thinking of asking me to eat, too?'

'Nothing was further from my mind,' she said.

'What a pity,' said Robert. 'I still want proof he's alive,' he added.

'He is,' said Dr McGregor, coming to the door. 'You've got our words for it.'

'That's what they all say. Sure he's not dead? He looked half-dead yesterday.'

'He's very much alive.'

'Oh.'

'You sound disappointed, Robert,' said Molly.

'Don't get me wrong, Mrs Henderson, I don't really want him dead but if he is, that means they might hang Darcy Pearson, and I can't wait for that!'

The old doctor sighed. 'Bad news always spreads quickly.'

'Geez, Dr Mac, it wouldn't be bad news if they hanged Pearson. When they do I'm going to apply to be a witness and cheer when they drop him.'

'You bloodthirsty little devil,' said the doctor.

'All right for you, you've never been bashed up and tortured by him! Bet that bloke in there you won't let me see would cheer the loudest.'

'That's as may be but, thank the good Lord, we don't have capital punishment these days.'

'My mum says that's a pity,' said Robert.

'Your long-suffering mother is probably looking at you when she says it,' said James McGregor. 'Come on then, I'll give you living proof that hanging isn't on the cards, at least for the moment! Two minutes, and not a second more.'

'Your generosity is succeeded only by your good looks, Dr Mac,' said Robert.

'I think you got a word wrong, Robert. Don't they teach you anything at that dratted school these days?'

'Not much, Dr Mac. Lead on, McDuff!'

'Humph! Didn't quite get that one right, either. Come on.'

Robert took a good close look at Jake. 'Hmm. Don't look too good to me, Dr Mac. If you want my professional opinion . . .'

'I don't remember asking for it, Robert. Jake, this wretched specimen of humanity is Robert Te Huia. He helped us dig you out of my poor hydrangeas and feels some degree of ownership. If you don't want him in here I'll take great pleasure in booting him out. Robert, this is Jacob Neill. Two minutes,' and the doctor left them.

'Gidday,' said Robert. 'You OK now?' And then he was tongue-tied.

Jake looked at Robert without blinking. He took in the broad, brown face, the mop of jet-black hair that was more than black, almost purple, and the half-grin, now somewhat shy. 'I think you came to see me yesterday,' he said. 'Thank you.'

'You talk funny. Poms do, eh?'

'No,' said Jake. 'But you do.' He smiled. Each looked at the other, assessing. They relaxed.

'They got that bugger and they reckon he nearly killed you. It's all over town and it's gonna be in the paper. Pity he didn't kill you 'cos then they might hang him . . . ' He realised what he'd said. 'Well, big pity he didn't kill someone I didn't like. What's it feel like?'

'What's what feel like?'

'Geez, you're a bit hard to understand,' and Robert spoke very slowly, loudly and deliberately. 'Do . . . you . . . feel . . . all . . . right?'

'I . . . am . . . not . . . deaf,' said Jake. 'I . . . speak . . . English!'

'If you say so, mate,' Robert grinned. 'What's gonna happen to you?'

'I don't know.'

'I'll come and see you again if the old bugger'll let me in. OK? My mum reckons he's the best doctor she's ever known, for all he's got a wicked temper.'

'Your mother is right on both counts, Ropata. Now . . . out!' Dr McGregor pointed.

'Mum says you're not to call me Ropata. It's Robert.'

90

'The day I do what your mother tells me, young man, will be the day I pop my clogs.'

'See what I mean, mate,' Robert grinned. He looked at Jake from the doorway. 'You'll be OK, even with Dr Mac as your doctor. See you tomorrow.'

'Don't count on the old bugger letting you in, Robert!' said Dr Mac.

IV

It took time.

There were nights when he couldn't sleep. At first there was pain. After the pain came intense irritation as his skin fought to mend itself. No matter how effective the doctor's treatments were, there were still times when Jake had to suffer. He endured without complaint to the extent that James McGregor, growling, said to him, 'If you want to scream, boy, then bloody scream. I've seen grown men whimper and moan from much less! Sometimes a good howl helps us all.'

After three or four nights, Molly Henderson returned to her own home. 'If you insist on keeping him here, Jim, that's fine and dandy. Just let me know if you need a break and he can come to me for a night or two. If you take my advice, you won't let it go on too long.' She looked at her old friend, but said nothing more.

'I know what I'm doing,' said James McGregor.

'Do you?' she smiled at him.

The days accumulated. And Jake began to wonder more about what was to happen to him. Where would he go? Could he just go?

He became increasingly friendly with Molly Henderson, indeed he spent more time with her than he did with the old doctor. He began pottering around, helping her in the kitchen, sharing cups of tea. He confided in her, telling the old woman the story of his family, the loss of his mother in what had been the worst air-raid to strike Coventry. Of how his father, a fireman and air-raid warden, had lost a leg not long after. Of his grandmother who had died and of the agonies of decision and indecision about what would be best for him and for his sister, Janice, and of how his father had decided a new life for the two of them would be better than what he could hope to provide. A new life in a new world.

Molly Henderson brought him pen and paper and he wrote to his father.

Dear Father,

I hope this finds you fit and well. I am having a good time and now stay in a town for a while. Well, it is not really a town, it is just a bit of a village. It has one street with a few shops and a post office and a bank and a library and other bibs and bobs. There is one school for the whole of the town. I do not know how long I am living here for. The farm where I was did not work out too good but I am fine. I think I might like to live in a town (or a village) but not on another farm but I suppose I will do what I am told because I have always done what I am told, ha ha. There is no need to worry.

The house I am staying in is a very big mansion sort of a house with more rooms than I can count. It is a doctor's house and his place of work. It is nearly as big as the orphanage run by the nuns where Janice and me lived after Gran had gone. But we don't have no nuns, ha ha. None nuns, ha ha ha ha.

I hope you get this letter. You can hop hop down to

the pub and read it them down there, hop hop ha ha.

Please write to me soon and tell me the news. Have you got a new leg yet? I hope it is a good one and better than the last one so that you hop even faster.

Your son

Jacob (Jake).

'Did Dr Mac's wife die?' he asked Molly Henderson, as he looked at a silver-framed photograph. An old photo, brown with years.

'Yes. That's the two of them. Goodness me, back in the twenties, I would think. Off for a day at the races.' Molly smiled. 'She loved her horses. He did, too. Particularly if it was a winner!'

'She died?'

'Yes. Soon after the war began. Quite suddenly.'

'Dr Mac doesn't say anything about her.'

'They were very happy,' she picked up the photo. 'Pauline, that was her name. She was lovely. My best friend. I guess that's why I'm here today — slaving my fingers to the bone running two houses' She laughed. 'And at my age!'

'Did they have children?'

'No. Now you get out to the kitchen, stoke up the range and get that kettle boiling. Mac'll be through for his morning tea at any moment. Scat! Off with you.'

'It itches,' he said to the doctor.

'Of course it itches. Doesn't mean to say you can scratch the hell out of it. God knows how you could have twisted yourself to scratch right up there. You a circus acrobat in an earlier life?'

'Yes,' said Jake. 'And a lion tamer.'

'Hah! Tell that to your dratted cat! You're not doing too good a job there, are you? Sure I can't drown the bugger for you?'

'You can drown him if you can catch him,' Jake grinned. Little Black Sambo gave Dr James McGregor a very wide berth. 'I think he's quite safe.'

'There's an old girl lives down the road from here, out in the country. Mrs Sykes. Funny old soul. Had she been born a few hundred years ago around where you come from, your ancestors would have burnt her at the stake as a witch. Must admit she looks like one. Now, modern medical science says I should say that what she gets up to is a load of old rubbish, but, for all that, I'm going to have her take a look at your back.'

'Why? Why would I want a witch looking at my back?'

'Because I say so, boy, and because she makes these potions and ointments from herbs and roots and bark and whatnot, and for all it's a load of old rubbish, it seems to work. We'll take a drive out there tomorrow afternoon, after I'm through here. Don't worry yourself if she never speaks a word to you. Least said soonest mended, is old Mrs Sykes' motto. Either that or she thinks silence is insurance against being burnt at that stake by young hooligans like you!' He smiled at Jake. 'Pop your cat in a bag. I'm told she's looking for a new fellow,' and he grinned more broadly. 'Last one fell off her broomstick. Was the tenth time it'd tumbled, so it didn't get up again.'

'So it's not my back you're interested in. You just want to get rid of my cat,' said Jake.

'Something like that. Now, then. You and me have to have a serious talk. Come on. We'll walk and talk around the garden, and I can smoke my pipe. Molly doesn't stop complaining if I smoke in the house. Smoke a pipe, lad?'

'No,' said Jake.

95

'Pity. Hope you don't smoke those other fool things.'

'Sometimes I do.'

'Oh, well. I guess you're grown-up enough. God knows, after what you've gone through in the last few years . . .' He looked the boy up and down. 'Bad for the wind, though, if you want to be a runner. And you've the build of a runner. Come on. You can point out the hydrangeas. You should know them by now. The ones you carelessly destroyed!'

They strolled the garden in silence before the doctor led the way back to the house and they sat together on the steps of the broad front veranda. 'Would you like to live here, boy?'

Jake looked at him. 'You mean here with you?'

'I'm not planning on moving out, lad, so you can have the whole darn place to yourself.'

'I didn't mean that.'

'Although it is hard for me to admit it, I am getting a bit long in the tooth. Seventy next birthday, dammit! Can't always do those things that need to be done. You'd work for your keep, mark my words. Mow the lawns, garden. Drive the car.'

'But I can't drive a car,' said Jake.

'I'll teach you,' said Dr Mac. 'You see, lad, the spirit's willing but the flesh is getting a bit weak. The old arthritis is taking its toll.' He held out a gnarled, knotted hand.

'I understand.'

'Yes. You're not too short in the old brain-box department. And that's another thing . . . you'd go to school.'

Jake breathed a sigh of contentment, closed his eyes, felt warm all over. Then chill struck. 'They wouldn't let me.'

'Who's they?'

'I don't know.' He took a stab. 'The police?'

James McGregor laughed. 'Don't worry about the authorities, laddie. Good God, boy! What are you, man or mouse?' He looked thoughtfully at Jake. 'I know what you mean, though. I haven't bothered you with all the ins and outs — but I've settled with the authorities already. You've been living here with me, quite legally, since a day or two after you plonked yourself in my hydrangeas and killed 'em. My legal wallahs saw to that. I guess it's a bit of a help when your best friend is also a judge. As we sit here talking, I am your legal guardian. For the time being, anyway.'

'You . . . you mean I've got no worries?'

'Didn't say that, did I? You've got me as a worry. What is it your best mate calls me — a bad-tempered old bugger? Don't promise you a bed of roses, young man.'

Jake wasn't listening. He had bent over, head almost between his knees, body shaking. When he finally raised his tear-soaked face, he stared directly at the old doctor. 'You're not a bad-tempered old bugger.'

'I take it that means your answer is yes. Come on, boy. It's not as bad as all that. Come here,' and he reached out a hand and pulled Jake towards him. 'Not too good at this. Here,' and he gave Jake a rough and ready hug. 'Dry those eyes. Come on inside and we'll drink to it. I'll have a whisky and you can have . . . dammit, you can have a whisky, too!'

He hadn't told Jake about the endless hours of argument with nurse and housekeeper. 'You don't know him! He doesn't know you!'

'He's fourteen and you're senile!'

'You'd have to be at least something of a parent! Really, Mac, it's not as if you've ever had any training.'

'Poor little kiddy like that and a doddering old fool! God knows,

Pauline'll be turning in her grave! What on earth d'you think you're playing at?'

'You know nothing of his background. Nothing at all!'

Then, finally, capitulation.

'He's a nice enough little chap. Sure he doesn't deserve better? I'll do what I can.'

And, 'Even this old pile of a place, and you besides, must be better than what he's had so far! He needs clothes. I'll make a list. No, I won't. You'll give me the money and I shall take him down to the city and fit him out! Oh, yes, I knew that'd make you blink!' A smile. 'We'll take young Robert as well. Make a day of it. Christmas is well nigh on us and I've still not got those curtain samples. Might even stay overnight.' And then a sly smile. 'You'd better start thinking of a Christmas tree, Mac. Can't have a kiddie in the house and no tree!'

From the far corners of his mind where he had hidden them away for safe keeping, Jake took out and brushed off his memories of his mother. It was safer, now, to let them surface, let them out. What surprised the boy was that while they still had the power to sadden him, the hurt and the pain they had once the generated had, somehow, lessened in intensity. At first this puzzled Jake until one day the realisation hit him that his mother had been gone from him for so long, and so much had happened to him in the years since that had changed his life and existence, for ill and then good. He knew that while he would never forget her, and that his memories of her would live within him forever, edges had started to blur. Memories were there in plenty, but, well, just sometimes it was getting a little hard to actually see her and hear her voice.

When he thought about his little sister, Janice, he knew that whatever memory she may still have of their mother would be fainter by far than his. Jake hoped with all his might that he would somehow get to see Janny before whatever memory she might still have of him was lost in the mists of time.

In the way of things, it was all a jumble. Hard, really, to separate the good from the bad. The once-a-year visits to Gran and the trips to the fairground near where she lived. The laughter and love on birthdays and high days and holidays. Somehow, though, it all got mixed up in some great big melting pot of good times . . . and the bad; air-raid sirens and shelters, blacked-out windows and bomb-sites, streets with this house and that house missing, sometimes three or four in a row so that those streets looked for all the world like giant gaping ugly mouths with some teeth still there, some decaying away — but too many missing. And then his father taking him to view the site of the little factory where his mother had worked until . . . Ahh! Some things were better hidden away . . .

V

Clarence Arthur Pearson was found not guilty on the charges he faced in the Magistrate's Court. The magistrate agreed with Pearson's lawyer that the man, a respected and hardworking member of the community with an otherwise unblemished record, had exerted no more than reasonable force in disciplining the boy. The magistrate also found that Pearson could in no way be held responsible for the actions that followed his departure from the worker's quarters.

Gary Walter Miller was found not guilty on the charges he faced in the same court. A normally decent and responsible young man, he had allowed himself to be carried away in the heat of the moment. His boyish actions, while inappropriate, were not necessarily unnatural. The magistrate said he placed considerable weight on the testimony of both Miller's employer and the president of the local rugby club as to Miller's worth as a young citizen. Gary Walter Miller shed tears of relief and joy.

Both verdicts were occasion for a cheer from the folk packed into the small, cramped, uncomfortable and very hot courtroom, most particularly those from the rural community.

Darcy Clarence Pearson was less fortunate. Despite heartfelt pleading from the expensive lawyer employed on his behalf by his parents, Pearson was found guilty on all of the serious charges he faced that day. The magistrate told Pearson that it was only the grace of God and sheer good luck that meant he was not facing a more serious charge; manslaughter at the least. The magistrate said it was a tragedy that a generally decent young man from a good family had allowed himself to be so carried away. Pearson was sentenced to borstal training, a term of up to two years, its length dependent on Pearson's own progress towards reform. The magistrate expressed the opinion that he would come out, at the end of the training as a wiser young man. Darcy Pearson also cried his eyes out.

Pearson was allowed five minutes with his parents before being packed in the back of a black wagon and then carted off to begin his sentence.

Jacob John Neill discovered that being a victim carried penalties of its own.

Neill's testimony could not be faulted. Two highly trained and hard-eyed lawyers couldn't budge him from the truth. He didn't embellish or exaggerate but was absolutely immovable in his opinion that he could not be held in any way responsible for what had happened to him. He looked straight ahead at all times and kept his eyes focussed either into the distance or on the three other witnesses called by the police; James Robert McGregor, medical practitioner, Margaret Beatrice Henderson, retired school teacher, and Robert William Te Huia, student. From time to time he drank from a glass of water, supplied by the court registrar on the orders of the magistrate. Supporting evidence offered by the police consisted, in the main, of a series of photographs of excellent quality, taken by Dr McGregor, of the injuries sustained by the victim. Additionally presented as evidence was a blood-soaked Harris tweed jacket, recovered a week following the events from beside the railways tracks near Tiakatahuna Siding, four or five miles from the town.

The only moments of sympathy for the victim came when the lawyer for Darcy Pearson, on examining the photographic evidence, suggested that the injuries were, more than likely, superficial and that now, some weeks later, full healing would have taken place. This was a lapse on the part of the lawyer because the magistrate then asked Jacob Neill to bare his back. Full healing had most certainly not taken place. Despite the best attentions of old Mrs Sykes, twisted, corded and still-livid flesh provided a ghastly map of the course of the events of that night.

Darcy Pearson's lawyer later asked Dr James McGregor whether, in his expert opinion, Jacob Neill could be a bleeder. The doctor said that he presumed the lawyer meant someone who bled profusely. The lawyer said that he considered it possible that Neill could well carry a similar genetic condition to that reputed to have been passed down to her descendants by Her late Royal Highness, Princess Beatrice of Great Britain and Northern Ireland. Dr McGregor said that to the best of his knowledge there was no connection between Jacob Neill and the late Princess — either by blood or medically.

The magistrate told Pearson's lawyer to stick to the point.

The only emotion shown by Jacob Neill came when the magistrate sent Darcy Pearson to borstal. He looked directly at the one who had caused him such agony and smiled broadly at his white-faced and trembling assailant.

There were those outside the court afterwards, mainly townsfolk, who patted Jake on the shoulder, gently, and said words like, 'Well done,' or 'Now you can put that behind you, laddie.'

But there were others, supporters of the Pearsons, fellow farmers and one or two largish young men who looked a bit like Gary Miller, who were in no way supportive of the victim.

'Gonna come out here, he's gotta learn to take his medicine.'

'Sad day when a bloke can't tell his worker what to do.'

'Decent folk, the Pearsons. Salt of the earth, for all old Clarrie can knock a few back.'

'Little pommie bastard.'

'He'll get sorted. Wouldn't want to be in his shoes when Darce gets out.'

'Thought he lost his shoes strugglin' through the swamp!' Laughter.

'Good for nothing pom. Can't take a bit of a laugh. Remember that calf we set on poor old Georgie, night before his wedding? Never had much to say about his wedding night, old Georgie.' More laughter.

'Old Darce, one of the best blokes I've ever played footie with. Good man to have on your side. Poor old Darce won't be gettin' much footie for a while. Team needs a bloke with a strong right arm!' Even more laughter.

'Come on, we'll go and sit down by old Mac's lily pond and throw stones at frogs and you can forget all about it,' said Robert Te Huia. They left the adults up at the house, talking through the events of the day, and lay in the warm sun of late afternoon. There were no frogs. 'You can't let it worry you any more. It's done. They put him away.'

'He'll get out.'

'You mean escape?'

'No. He can only be there two years at the very most.'

'Seems like a helluva long time to me,' said Robert. He looked at Jake. 'You got a lot of things to look forward to now. We're goin' to the city with old Molly. Then there's Christmas, the holidays and then you've got school.'

'Don't want to go to school any more,' said Jake.

'Oh, yeah? Since when?'

'Since this afternoon,' said Jake. 'I'll just stay here and do my work for Dr Mac.'

'Oh, yeah. You mean hide?'

'Can't hide doing these lawns. They're big as a bloody park.'

'You know what I mean.'

They lay, side by side, face down in the sun. The warmth of the sun was bliss on Jake's back and, slowly, his mood lightened. 'You heard the things they were saying when we got out of the court. I know why. I'm the outsider and I got one of them in trouble. As I see it, they'll make me pay.'

'Forget them. Those ones mouthing off outside the court, most of 'em aren't from here in town,' said Robert, patiently. 'Just sometimes, it's like it's two different places. It's the rich ones have the land and the farms and the cows, the sheep. You know, there's only one rich one here in town. Reckon you know who that is! None of that lot mouthing-off even go to our school.'

'They'd have kids who did, or brothers, or something.'

'Yeah. But just one or two. Mainly the farm-worker kids. The farm-owner kids get sent away to school because of two things,' said Robert.

'What two things?'

'They think it's better,' he grinned. 'And it wouldn't be hard for anywhere else to be better than Weatherley District High School. I dunno what you think our school is like. It's just a little place with about fifty kids in the secondary department. If it makes you feel any better, I'm the biggest one there.' He grinned some more.

104

'What's the other reason.'

'They're so bloody dumb their parents hide 'em away so's no one else will ever find out. They're so dumb they go straight from school to the loony bin.'

'The loony bin?'

'The mad house. The mental hospital.'

Jake laughed. 'Now I know you're joking.'

'Yeah. Well it made you laugh, eh? Quick! There's a frog. Get it!'

'No,' said Jake. 'Leave it alone. It's not doing you any harm.'

'That's not the point,' said Robert, firing a stone and missing.

'You want to bash me up and kill frogs. You're the same as Darcy Pearson.'

'Comes from growin' up round here. Let's have a smoke. I find that in moments of great stress it helps your nerves. Mind you, if my mum caught me, then I'd really be in great stress.'

'I think I'd like to meet your mum. You terrified of her?'

'Hell, yes. You'd be, too, if she was your mother,' said Robert, feelingly. 'Here I am. Grown up. I'm fifteen! And she still scares the wits out of me.'

'I think she might be the only person who does,' said Jake.

'No. Dr Mac does, too. Just I never let him see it. It's better for him that way.'

'Tell me more about the school. Would we be in the same class?' Jake asked.

'I dunno how dumb you are, do I?'

'Are you a genius?'

'Yes,' Robert smoked. 'Depends on what old Baldy Brass-arse says when Dr Mac brings you along. He's the boss. That's not his real name.'

'Oh, isn't it?'

Robert grinned at him. 'Don't get clever with me, Pommie. I'll be in the fifth form. I'm doing School Cert next year. There's only about five of us and I think old Baldy just might put you in there, too, even if you are a bit younger. Or he might put you with the fourth form. Who knows? I'll have a word with him if you like. Takes my word for everything, and my advice, does old Baldy,' he was grinning more broadly.

'Probably because you've said you'll bash him up, too, if he doesn't.'

'You've got it,' said Robert. 'You're gettin' to know me.'

'Yes, well, Mrs Henderson told me that given half a chance you'd run the town.'

'Given half a chance? Wait till I see her! I run it already,' he picked up a stone, fired it at a lily-pad. 'Gotcha! Got that one.'

'No you didn't.'

'Not the bloody frog. I got the flower,' said Robert. He turned on his side and faced Jake. 'You feel a bit better now?'

'Why do you want to be friendly with me?

'God Almighty, you ask odd questions. Why? I dunno. Look, mate, remember I just told you there would be four or five of us in the fifth form? Well, the other four are all girls — and you should see them! It's just about all boys in the fourth form — and you should see them, too! As my mum says, any port in a storm. You, Pommie Jake, are a gift from the gods.'

'Never been called that before,' said Jake, now smiling.

'Well don't get used to it. I won't be sayin' it again,' said Robert.

In the weeks leading up to Christmas, Jake found his life settling into a routine. As his strength returned he took on those jobs around the place he knew James McGregor wanted him to do. After milking a herd of cows, it was easy. He enjoyed his work — the lawns, weeding the gardens, raking the gravel of the driveway into a variety of patterns. A quick learner. The old man only had to tell him anything once and it was done, neatly, and precisely in the way he'd been shown. He continued to help Molly around the house, cleaning windows and, as he grew fitter, scaling up a ladder to hang the new curtains that arrived from the city. Indeed, anything he was asked to do, he did. Quick, willing, efficient.

The trip to the city came and went, and Jake's wardrobe expanded.

Two other things happened that made Jake think he was living a dream. 'Mac says you can have whatever room you like, love, but it's time to move out of the little one near the surgery. He uses that occasionally if anyone needs a bed in a hurry.'

'Like me, or like someone having a baby?' Jake asked.

'It's been known,' she smiled. 'You can have any of the ones upstairs or you can have the little one out behind the kitchen. Take my advice and . . .'

'I'll have the little one,' said Jake, firmly.

'Well, that was my advice, had you given me half a chance. It's snug and warm and cosy in winter and it's got that nice French-door out into the garden, looking over the pond. Nice and private and got its own lavatory and a basin. Let's go and sort it out. Can't remember when it was last used.'

It might be a little room to these people but it was almost as big and twice as grand as the home in Coventry where he'd grown up — and shared with his mother, father and baby sister! 'It's as big and grand as Buckingham Palace,' he grinned at Molly.

'If you say so,' she laughed.

'Nearly as big as our whole house at home,' he said.

'And what was that like, love? Your old home?' she bustled about the room, pushing boxes aside and opening up windows.

'It's gone now,' he said, quietly. 'It's gone . . . it went . . . it was early one . . . we got out . . .'

'There's no need, Jake . . . Silly old me, I should have thought,' said Molly, moving towards Jake as if to take the boy in her arms.'

Jake smiled, but moved away from her slightly, 'There's no need,' he said. 'It wasn't much of a house. Not really. It's not . . . it wasn't where my mum was . . . it's all right. You know what I remember about it most?'

'No need to say anything if you don't want to,' said Molly.

'The big table we had. Big, big table. Took up a lot of room. My dad had made it strong, see. Put steel bits all underneath . . .'

'Oh, yes. Why was that?'

'For when we didn't have time to get out and run to the shelter. The sound . . . I always remember the sound. Sort of whistly wee sick windy sound in the air, and my dad's ears were so good. He'd always hear them. Then it wasn't a whistle any more, just a sort of waiting nothing, and then somewhere outside *Boom!* And noise, so much noise. Noise and smell and quite often, the smoke . . . Bloody old Jerry again, eh? And me and Janny and Mum and Dad under the table. Me and Janny would be thrown under, just chucked under, it hurt sometimes and Janny howling her head off, me, too. Just thrown under and Mum and Dad in on top. Not every day . . .'

'That's enough, love,' said Molly.

Jake's hand came up to his mouth to cover his nervous giggle. 'Then, when it was all over, we'd be dragged out, and you know what?'

Molly looked at him, and smiled slightly, 'Tell me, lad, and then let that be an end to it. I'm sorry I . . . '

'When we got out, Janny and me, Mum would often, nearly always, whack us both,' he rubbed his bottom. 'Hard, too, she'd lay into us. What do you think of that, eh?' But he didn't give Molly a chance to reply. 'Not that long ago I suddenly sort of knew why she did it. I realised why.'

'Time for a cuppa,' said Molly Henderson. 'Yes, indeed.'

'Better get things on a business-like footing, lad,' said James McGregor, after dinner one night. 'You're doing well in more ways than I care to mention. Knew I hadn't made a mistake, regardless of what the old biddies told me.'

'What did the old biddies tell you?'

'None of your business. Here,' and he took a ten-shilling note from his pocket and handed it to Jake. 'You've earned it.'

'I can't take your money. . . you look after me and I don't need the money. . . '

'You'll take it, if I say so. You've earned it several times over. Not scared of hard work and not a moment of complaint, and no one knows better than I do that your bloody back is still not fully better, still plays merry hell. Sit down!' An order.

'Um . . . ' Jake sat.

'Listen, boy, and stop interrupting me. You live here by my choice. I keep you. I will see that you're educated to the best of that damn school's ability. I will feed you and clothe you, but you are not my slave. If I choose to pay you on top of anything else, that is my decision. What you do with what you earn, that's up to you. Spend it, if you will. Spend some, save some. Save the lot. We'll open a bank account for you. You'll need money for your future.'

'That was a long speech,' said Jake. 'Thank you.' He took the ten shillings. 'There's no need to give me any more.'

'You stupid little bugger. You'll get that much once a week.'

'I knew that,' said Jake, grinning.

'You're spending too much time with that wretched Robert. Learning his wicked ways.' The doctor smiled back at him. 'Take my advice and get your money in the bank otherwise it'll all be going down the drain on fast women and booze.'

Jake laughed. 'I know where you get the booze around here but I haven't seen any fast women. They're all very slow, like Mrs Henderson.'

'I'll tell her you said that,' said James McGregor. 'Now, I don't want you falling out of your skin with gratitude or telling me you can't possibly take it, but I've got you a bicycle. Call it your Christmas present if it makes you feel better. Handy for running errands, and you'll need it for school.'

Jake's grin spread right across his face. He said nothing.

'Well, what d'you say?'

'You said to say nothing,' said Jake.

'Fair enough. Your Cheshire cat grin says it all. Last, and not at all least, time you did a bit of reading. Haven't seen you with a book since you got here and, God knows, this house has more books than the town library.'

Jake's grin had gone.

'You can read? Of course you can read. What's up?'

'I can't find my glasses. I don't know where they went.'

'You stupid little devil. Stupid old devil, too, for not thinking. You wear glasses?'

'Yes. Just for reading.' Turning his ten-shilling note over in his

110

hand, he added, 'I'll save up to get some more.'

'Like hell you will. I shall see to that. Half a dozen pairs somewhere, floating around in the surgery . . . Hmm, short-sighted?'

'Yes.'

'We'll get 'em tested and sort out a pair of specs for you. Your ten bob a week is certainly not for things like that.'

'Can I go and see my bike now?'

'Certainly you can, but kindly use the King's English,' said Dr Mac.

'May I go and see my bike now?'

'Yes, you may go. Good lad.'

Later, in his own room, he sat on the side of his bed, holding his ten-shilling note in his hands, turning it over and over. A feeling of absolute well-being filled him. He stood up and looked out into the moonlit garden. 'Shit hot!' he whispered, using one of Robert Te Huia's favourite expressions. He opened the French door and went out onto the terrace outside his room. Jumping up and down with absolute delight and glee and joy he used every other bad or foul word he could think of to celebrate his great good fortune.

VI

Just before Christmas he began to see Gary Miller, almost every day it seemed. At first Jake thought he was imagining that the other was following him but, as the time passed, it seemed that, most days, he would spot Miller. The once daily trips out to old Mrs Sykes had dropped off to twice a week. The healing was as complete as it would ever be and no amount of massage would erase the last of his scars. On one occasion Gary Miller sat on his motorbike, fifty yards or so from the gates of the old woman's cottage. He made no approach. As he rode the couple of miles home again, Miller gunned his bike past him not once, but three times. Jake, head down, biked on. Another time he saw him, again on his motorbike, outside the gates to the doctor's house. One day he walked down to the post office for Molly Henderson. There was no option but to pass the garage where Gary Miller worked, but Jake crossed to the other side of the street to avoid the place. No sign of Miller. Not then. But on his way back, there he was, leaning against the petrol pump, arms folded, his eyes on Jake, staring.

He tried to put it out of his mind, but it bothered him. No more so than one night when he read late, very late, curled up on his bed, with Little Black Sambo stretched out beside him. Near midnight, he discarded the temporary glasses given him by Dr Mac, stood and stretched, then walked over to the French doors, wearing only his underpants. He opened the doors and breathed in the night air. There was a figure standing stock-still in the moonlight down by the lily pond. Jake closed his eyes, rubbed them, shook his head and looked again. There was no one there. It was his imagination. There was no way Miller had been standing in the middle of James McGregor's garden. No way.

Christmas hummed and buzzed as much as it possibly could in the home of an old doctor who worked a full day, every day, right up until the event. 'As old Charlie Dickens had someone saying; Scrooge, if memory serves, *Christmas is humbug*. We'll take a little holiday in January, boy, just you'n me, if I can find a locum.'

'What's a locum?'

'Generally some young saw-bones, still wet behind the ears and fresh out of medical school who could do with a spot of work. What do you make of Christmas? You a Christmas sort of feller?'

'No,' said Jake, firmly. Most certainly not in this upside down place at the bottom of the world where it was the middle of a very hot summer. 'We didn't go in for Christmas very much, well not for a long time. We never had much money, and when the war came it wasn't easy.'

'Molly tells me you and she have sewn up a nice parcel of bits and pieces to send to your old man. Bit of tucker he might not otherwise get.'

'Yes. The lady at the post office said it wouldn't get there on time but that doesn't matter,' Jake smiled. 'My old man will enjoy them whenever they get there. I paid for the things.'

'Good man.'

'Mrs Te Huia said Robert was to bring me to their place so she could say Happy Christmas,' Jake blushed slightly. 'And have a

113

little Christmas drink. If that's all right. Is that all right?'

'Of course it's all right, lad. You don't have to ask me. Don't you hit the sherry bottle too hard,' he chuckled. 'I don't want that grinning brown face leading you astray. Not that his mother would let him! Fine woman. A pity about her son, poor soul.'

Jake laughed out loud. 'I think you like Robert very much indeed.'

'Do you just? Oh, and one other thing, Jacob, my boy.'

'What's that?'

'Christmas and everything, well, if you want to go to church, you just sort it out for yourself and take off if you see fit. Me? Well, lad, no use beating around the bush, I'm a bloody heathen.'

Jake looked at the old man and a broad smile spread across his face. 'I'm a bloody heathen, too, Dr Mac,' he said. 'We can be a couple of bloody heathens together.'

'Good man. And don't bloody swear.'

'I only bloody swear if you bloody swear, Dr Mac.'

'No need to copy everything I do. Thought you said you spent some time with the nuns?'

'They took Janice and me when my gran died and after Mum had gone . . .' He was quiet for a moment. 'They were quite good. I went to the brothers' school.' He smiled. 'They could bloody swear! The bloody brothers!'

'Not surprised, poor devils, if they had a school full of the likes of you. Come on, let's get inside. Time for my whisky, and don't be looking at me like that, you're not getting one!'

'I've been telling him for weeks to bring you round and introduce you. It's all 'Jake this' and 'Jake that' and not enough manners in him to see that we meet. Sit down and help yourself to a mince pie;

they're fresh from the oven.' Mrs Te Huia bustled around her tiny kitchen. 'Come on now. Eat up. I've not made them for myself.'

The woman fitted her kitchen — small and bird-like, a head shorter than her son. Jake was amazed. This little creature controlled Robert with a rod of iron? He couldn't believe it! 'They're very nice mince pies, Mrs Te Huia. Thank you.'

'Have another,' she said, pushing the plate at him, 'Help yourself, lad.'

'That's my mum,' said Robert. 'She likes people to eat.'

'It shuts them up is why,' said his mother. 'Seems I failed with you, though,' she smiled at her son.

'What d'you think, Jake?' Robert stood up, gave his mother a hug and dwarfed her. She pushed him off. 'As like as two peas in a pod? My mum'n me?'

'Get away with you, boy,' she said.

'Except I'm brown and she's white. Pale as a sheet. Poor old Mum!' and he gave her a hug.

'And I'm a good host and you're a bad one. Offer the lad a drink.'

'Beer, Jake?' asked Robert.

'A cup of tea is what I meant, as well you know. You'll not be offering the poor lad hard liquor in my house.'

'It's Christmas, Mum. Beer isn't hard liquor and I know you got some.'

'For your uncle when he comes. And I don't know where the dickens they've got to.' She peered out of the window. 'Late, always late.'

'That's us Maoris. Time to us is a different dimension. You should know that, Mum,' and he pointed to a large, oak-framed photograph hanging on the wall. 'That was my dad,' he said to Jake. 'In his uniform, before he went away.'

The picture showed a broadly smiling soldier, an older image of the boy now sitting at the table. 'What Robert might not have told you is that he was killed, near the beginning of the war. North Africa. Second battalion, not the Maori one. We miss him,' Mrs Te Huia said simply.

'Robert didn't tell me,' said Jake, not knowing what else to say.

'You've been through enough without me telling you that. I would have. You lost your mum. I lost my dad. You sort of lost your dad, too.'

'Go and get a bottle of beer, Bobby, and bring me that bottle of sherry I was saving, the nice South African one with the deer on it. Maybe we could have just a little drink and blow your uncle and aunty for being late.' Mrs Te Huia got back to bustling.

They wandered the one-horse town together, Robert and Jake. The post office, the hotel, the bank, three churches, the library and the council office and the shops — Jake had already counted the whole eleven of them. Night was coming on. A hot night. A still night. The only evidence of any life, apart from themselves, was the hum of industry from the dairy factory that overlooked the town. They parked themselves in the band rotunda that sat in a small and dusty garden at the intersection of the two main streets. 'Not even Mum's eyes can see around a corner, I hope,' said Robert. 'We'll have a smoke.'

'She's a very nice lady, your mother,' said Jake, not knowing what else to say.

'You wouldn't say that if she'd chased you with a wooden spoon for the whole of your life,' said Robert, with great feeling.

'Poor little Bobby.'

'Don't you dare call me that.'

'OK, Bobby. I like your uncle and auntie, too.'

'They're OK. I'll take you out to their place one day. They've got a farm. Only Maoris left round here with a bit of land.'

'A cow farm?' Jake asked.

'Dairy farm. Yep. I've got to go out at the weekend and help him do the chooks for Christmas dinner. Want to come and give us a hand?' Robert asked.

'What d'you mean do the chooks for Christmas dinner?'

'Wring their necks, pluck 'em and take their guts out. Don't mind the first bit and the last bit but the plucking takes for ever. Want to come?'

'No, thanks,' said Jake, with some feeling.

'Well, it's gotta be done. Only time we ever get chicken is at Christmas. My mum can cook chooks real good.'

'Well, I suppose, if you do need a helping hand. . . ' Jake was reluctant.

'It's OK. You couldn't kill a chook, anyway. You'd cry.'

'I would not,' said Jake. 'As you say, it's got to be done.' He laughed. 'It's just that I'd rather have someone else do it. I'm not soft.'

'Oh, yeah? Look at that horrible kitten of yours. Any sensible bloke would've finished that sod off the day it was born!' Little Black Sambo liked Robert Te Huia as little as he liked Dr James McGregor. 'Don't worry. I'm not gonna touch him. And uncle and me can do the chooks. We always have,' he sighed. 'Guess we always will,' he sighed again. 'I'll end up an old man, still livin' round here and good for nothing except killing old hens at Christmas. That'll be my life.'

'It's very sad, Bobby,' grinned Jake. 'Very, very sad.'

117

It was the strangest Christmas Jake had ever experienced. James McGregor worked through until Christmas Eve and was on call all Christmas Day. As the only doctor for miles around, neither high day nor holiday made a great deal of difference. As he said, 'If a baby wants to arrive on Christmas Day it will. Right back to when the damn fool season got started. We can blame the Infant Jesus!'

Since the death of his wife he had spent the day with Molly Henderson and her family; a daughter, son-in-law and three small children. Gifts were exchanged, tempers frayed, the elaborate roast meal was cooked and eaten on the hottest afternoon of the year. Everyone, except the grandchildren who were busy playing with and breaking each other's small gifts, took a late afternoon snooze before gathering around the radio for the Christmas message from the King before sitting down for a further feast.

Jake's fortune was extended by a one-pound note from his guardian, a shirt from Molly Henderson and handkerchiefs from the grandchildren and their parents. He had pondered hard on what he could possibly give either Dr Mac or Molly. The shops in Weatherley didn't offer a wide assortment when it came to gifts. In the end he settled on a cup and saucer for Molly and a book for James McGregor. 'It's a good juicy murder one and you've got lots of them.'

'Thank you, Jacob. A sensitive gift for Christmas.' He looked at the book. 'Who d'you reckon did it? The doctor?'

'More than likely,' said Jake. 'They do, you know. I read all about Dr Crippen.'

VII

On Boxing Day James McGregor drove himself down to the city. 'Going to spend the day with a couple of old cronies. I'll probably spend the night and be back lunchtime or so tomorrow. I won't take you, lad, you can stay with Molly if you want.' He gave a short laugh. 'If I were you I'd have a nice quiet day to meself, pottering around here. Have an idle day. You've done enough work for two men. Lie out in the sun, or whatever it is you feel like doing. Shouldn't be any calls. I've told the exchange where I'll be and they'll put 'em on to the hospital or, if needs be, refer them to young Sandy over at Pukeonake.'

It felt good being by himself. It was almost as if the whole place was his very own property. The big wooden house, its grand verandas, the sweeping driveway and the old trees and the park-like gardens. In a way it was all his. This was his home. Just looking around him, revelling in it all, he felt, for the very first time, remarkably secure. He was happy, living here with this funny, crusty old codger of a doctor. The old man made him feel like a young man — and that felt just right!

Jake didn't obey James McGregor. He mowed the lawns and raked the driveway before he lay in the sun down by the lily pond. He made himself lunch. Bread and raspberry jam. More bread and

119

raspberry jam — and a cup of tea. He curled up on a sofa, out on the veranda, read a book, snoozed.

In the late afternoon he went outside, down to the little lake with its lily-pads, iris and croaking frogs. He fell asleep in the sun.

Jake woke with a start, turned face up, lay on his back. There, standing above him, staring down at him, was Gary Miller. 'Get away. Get away from me! Get out!' Jake yelled. He trembled, sprang into a crouch, arms crossed over his bare chest, a pathetic, protective reaction. 'I'll call . . . I'll get . . . '

'There's no one to call 'cos the old doc's out. I know. You're by yourself. I been watching all day,' Gary said quietly.

Miller's words made it worse. Jake backed off in a half crawl, slowly. 'Please go away. Leave me alone.' He was cornered.

'I gotta talk to you,' said Gary Miller. His hand came up to his face and rubbed his brow. 'I gotta talk. I'm not gonna hurt you. Please believe me.'

There was something in Miller's voice that made Jake relax his guard a fraction. He looked more closely into the face he remembered so painfully well. He remembered, as if it were just a moment ago, the sneering, jeering look and the grip of those big hands.

'Please just listen to me for a minute,' said Miller, pleading.

'What d'you want?' Jake was less fearful.

'Come back here and sit on your rug. I won't touch you. Don't you be scared.'

'I'm not scared,' Jake lied.

'Yes you are,' said Gary. 'I'll sit here and not move.' And he did.

Jake relaxed a degree more. 'What d'you want coming in here?' His confidence increased. 'You've got no right!' And then all of a sudden he realised there was nothing to fear. 'You bastard! You cruel, bully bastard!'

Gary turned slightly to look at Jake, his face serious. He spoke levelly, with no rise or fall to his voice. 'You can say to me what you like 'cos you're right.'

'What?'

'I looked at you while you were asleep and I looked at your back.'

Jack pulled the rug around him and sat, staring straight ahead. 'Yeah?'

'And I thought I done that to you, sort of in a way. I know I didn't really do that bit but it's been in my mind since that day in the court when they made you show what was done and now I can't even sleep.'

Jake looked at him. 'I hope you never bloody sleep again.' He saw tears on Miller's face. 'You sook! What are you crying for? Nobody hit you.'

'I can't get it out of my mind.'

'Good. I hope you never do.'

'I gotta say these things. I been tryin' to say them to you for weeks.'

'What things?'

'No one'll talk to me, almost no one in the whole town, and my mum says I'm disgusting. I'm tryin' to get outa here and get a job down the city. I had to see you before I go.' Gary Miller dug in his pocket and found cigarettes and matches. 'D'you want one?' His hand trembled.

'I don't smoke.'

'Yes you do. I seen you with Te Huia in the band rotunda just before Christmas. You were laughin' and jokin' with him.'

'So? I can laugh with people who don't torture me.'

'I come here today to say I am very sorry for what I done. I know it was wrong. The more I think about it the worser it is.' Gary spoke at length. He was quiet for a couple of seconds. 'How's your cock?'

Jake blinked. 'It still works.'

'That's good,' said Gary, seriously. 'Dunno what you'd do if it didn't. What Darce'n me did was very wrong. It's OK to have a bit of fun with a dumb calf or a few cats or shoot rabbits and shit, but what we did to you . . . '

Jake interrupted. 'No. I think you've got some more thinking to do. It's not OK to have a bit of fun with a dumb calf. That poor little calf got it worse than I did. I'm not soft. I don't care if calves get turned into meat or shoes or whatever . . . so long as they don't get treated bad before it happens. There's no need to be cruel to them.'

'You think so?' Miller sounded surprised. 'Never thought like that before.'

'And I don't think you are sorry for what you did. You're sorry for yourself, with no one talking to you and everyone thinking you're disgusting.'

'If that's what you think,' Gary stood. 'I had to come and say it. I'm very sorry.' He turned to leave and began walking away.

Jake got to his feet. 'Hey!'

Miller stopped, turned. 'What?'

'You can come back,' said Jake. 'I don't know what you want me to say. I'll never forget what you and that bugger did to me. I know you weren't the main one but you were happy to follow what he started.' He sighed again. 'You're sorry now but I know you weren't sorry back then. You enjoyed it. You thought what you did to me was funny.'

'I suppose you're right,' said Gary. 'Can I stay and just talk? Nuthin' else to do.'

'I can't stop you.'

'See, Darce is me mate. I'll be there for him when he comes out of prison, but I'll tell him all this, too. I will. I tried to write him a letter, but it wouldn't work.'

'What do you mean, it wouldn't work?'

'Couldn't get the words down, so I never done it, really. But I was gonna say in it what I just said to you.' He stuck out his right hand. 'Shake?' he asked.

Jake's palm sweated. With all his heart and soul he wanted to say no. He rubbed his sweating palm on his shorts and breathed very hard. 'All right,' he said reluctantly and stuck out his hand. It was a strange sensation.

Jake wanted Gary Miller to be gone, but the other sat down again, lit another cigarette and relaxed. 'It's nice here. You sure as hell lucky old Mac likes you. Doesn't like too many people. Never liked me.'

Jake was pleased to hear that. 'Why not?'

'Dunno. That your cat I heard about?'

Suddenly Jake tensed again as Little Black Sambo strolled towards them. 'Yes,' he said, shortly.

'Ugly bugger,' said Gary, pleasantly.

'No he's not,' said Jake.

'Yes he is. Here kitty, kitty,' and Gary Miller extended a hand.

'You keep your . . . ' and then Jake relaxed as Little Black Sambo ignored him completely, walked straight to Gary, purred loudly and enjoyed being stroked. 'Hell's bells!' said Jake. 'You're the first person other than me he's ever gone to. Now I know he's mad.'

'He trusts me,' said Gary, pleased with himself.

'Then he's one dumb cat,' said Jake.

'I don't knock off every cat I come across. Well, only some. This one's OK, except for the way he looks,' Gary picked up the kitten. 'You better get old Mac to whip the nuts off him soon. You want me to do it?' he offered. 'I think I just about know how.' He scrutinised Little Black Sambo's private parts.

'No thank you,' Jake said. 'I'll have one of your smokes.'

'Good idea,' said Gary. 'Then you can tell me about the war and what it was like and them bombs comin' down. See any dead people?'

'Yeah,' Jake sighed. 'Everywhere, and bombs all the time.'

'You mean real piles of 'em?'

'Yeah. Couldn't walk down the street, not that there was much of a street left, what with the bombs, and the bits that were left, well, you couldn't see them, either, because of all the dead bodies.'

'Aw, great. Bloody great,' said Gary, beaming broadly. 'Tell me some more. I got plenty more smokes. Did ya see some Nazis or a Gestapo? See them buggers get strung up on telephone poles?'

Jake sighed, and settled down. 'Yeah,' he said. 'Up and down our street. All the time.'

'D'you ever get to see old Hitler?'

'No,' said Jake. 'He didn't come round our way.'

VIII

Jake wrote home.

My dear Dad,

This is just to tell you that I am well and I have not heard from you for a very long time. I hope this finds you fit and well and hopping around like a bee in a bottle. It is summer here and it seems to be summer forever. It is so hot you wouldn't believe.

I am keeping busy with everything I have to do like the lawns and they are as big as any park at home and I have helped Molly the housekeeper bottle nearly a hundred bottles of peaches for eating in the winter. Dr Mac says I work too bloody hard. Those are his words. He pays me well and I am saving. I got a bank account now at the Post Office in town and a little book that shows how much I save. I will soon be a millionaire ha ha. Well it might take a million years ha ha.

My big news is I can now drive a car. It has not been easy and I am sad to say that Dr Mac is not a good teacher. He is the worst teacher of anything I have ever had and you should just hear him and what he says when I get it wrong. It is not made easy with me not being too tall and it's a bit hard to see out the front window of the car. I don't know why he wants me to drive him around if I am such a bad driver (he says) and give him fatal heart attacks. (I don't. It is all in his mind.) He wants me to be the driver if he has calls to go to because of his arthritis. This is a big problem for Dr Mac, his arthritis. He says driving the big car is just too much for his hands and wrists. Nurse Barbara also drives him but I will do the weekends and after school when school starts. The car is a Buick and it is dark blue. It is certainly a big bugger (Dr Mac's word for it). It is the biggest car in this town. I get to keep it clean and polished but my friend Robert says he will polish if I pay him two bob. Ha ha he is not getting my money.

This is a long letter.

I have to have a cushion to sit on to see out the front window. I don't need a licence, not yet, but I will get one soon. It is all right for the driving if Dr Mac is in the car with me. I might as well go on because Dr Mac says if he sees me doing any more work today he will boot my backside. He would have to catch me first ha ha.

I wish I knew what happened to our Janice. I had some times when I couldn't think much about her but I do now and I wonder where she is. Dr Mac says we are going to go to Wellington and see the authorities. I think she must be all right. I hope she's not on a farm but I don't think she would be because she's a bit little to be much use.

I hope you are pleased to know that I can swim now. My friend Robert taught me that and he is a better teacher than Dr Mac. I have told him I will teach him to drive the car when Dr Mac's not looking. We swim in a river out by his uncle's farm which is a good long (hot) bike ride. It's good fun and we shoot rabbits him and me out on that farm. There are thousands of the buggers (Robert's word) out there and are a big pest. It is a pity I think rabbits are quite nice but I tell myself they are just pretty rats with fluffy tails and then shoot. I am a good shot and they fall stone dead most of the time. We don't eat them much out here not like at home. I think it is because there are so many sheep and we eat them instead. We are always eating sheep in New Zealand and we eat meat every day, I think because there are so many to eat. We would never get through them all ha ha.

By the time you get this I will be back at school. It is a worry for me because I don't think I will like that but I have got to go because I am not fifteen for a while yet.

I have just looked at all of what I have written to you. It is so long that I have used some swear words under my breath but I won't write them because I don't want to shock you ha ha.

With love from your son,

Jacob Neill.

'Ah, this the little pommie feller of yours, Mac? The one I've heard so much about,' said George Gibbons, headmaster.

'Still got you in harness, George? Isn't it time they put you out to pasture?'

'Told 'em that seven years back when they dragged me out of happy retirement. First crop of young blood coming through now; these rehab blokes they've been training. None seem to want to come here. Too many took off who never came back.'

Jacob John Neill was enrolled — and then sent home for a few weeks when an outbreak of polio closed all schools.

'What d'you make of old Baldy?' Robert asked Jake.

'He was OK. He talked to Dr Mac all the time. Mac says I've got to stop working so much and just do the lawns so I've got time to read and do some writing.'

'If you don't have to do so much work for old Mac, you'n me can go out to the farm more often, swim and shoot rabbits. You're a crook swimmer but you're quite a good shot.'

'I'll do the reading,' said Jake. 'Mr Gibbons says I might have some catching up to do. He's going to put me in the fourth form because of all the changes I've had.'

'Old Baldy Brass-arse wouldn't know the time of day,' said Robert. 'Most of the time he sits in his office with the door locked, drinking whisky.'

'If the door's locked, how d'you know?'

'Climbed up and spied on him through the window one day when I was in the third form. Whew, he whacked me that day!' Robert rubbed his backside.

'I never know when you're telling the truth and when you're not,' said Jake.

'God help me, but I am the most truthful person you'll ever meet,' Robert grinned.

'Then God help me,' Jake grinned back at him.

Jake went unwillingly to school. Molly Henderson turned up early to send him off on his first day. She checked his uniform, navy-blue and new, set his cap straight on his sun-bleached fair head, made him pull up the socks that prickled in the sweltering heat of early autumn, made sure he had his cut lunch. Neither she nor James McGregor could get a smile onto his face. He'd eaten breakfast and vomited the lot down the lavatory bowl. Empty of stomach, and almost empty of hope, he biked off.

Feeling several hundred percent better he biked home again at the end of the day.

'So?' Molly Henderson waited on the veranda.

Jake smiled broadly. 'I don't know what I was worried about.'

'I told you so.'

'And I'm in the fifth form — with Robert.'

'Told George Gibbons you would be. No problems?' she queried.

He knew what she meant. 'No. One or two funny looks when I first got there, but that could've been for anything.'

'Oh ye of little faith,' the old woman smiled at him. 'Come on. There's a nice cuppa just brewed and Mac'll be finished presently and want to hear about it all. Let me tell you, he was as worried as you this morning. You should have heard him after you'd gone. He was all for taking off and dragging you back!'

Like a duck to water, Jake Neill took to school. There was really very little not to take to! Robert had been absolutely right — there were only fifty in the secondary department. Indeed Jake was the fiftieth. There were twenty-six in the third form, nineteen in the fourth, five, including Jake, in the fifth and one lonely sixth former.

By the end of the first day he'd discovered who controlled the school in all ways other than academic; his mate, Robert Te Huia.

Robert's control was absolute and neither Lance, the lonely sixth-former, nor the four teachers who ran the place seemed to have any problem with this.

'I've got you down for the First XI. Well, it's the only XI. You can bowl?'

'I don't think I want to play cricket,' said Jake.

'Well, you will. Come winter you'll be in the First XV. You have to. It's either you or Maisie, she's the big one in our class, and she could pass for a bloke any day.'

'What's the First XV?'

'What?' Robert was amazed, 'Footie.'

'Soccer? Fifteen?'

Robert's mirth knew no bounds and he rolled around on the grass before putting Jake right. 'And because of your first-hand experience, you'll be the sergeant when we do cadets on Fridays.'

Jake was rather confused. 'What is cadets and what first-hand experience?'

'We gotta make the most of you. You're the only one in the whole school, apart from Brass-arse, with first-hand experience of real war and I think Mum told me his one was the Crimean with Florence Nightingale. I think old Florence might have been his first girlfriend. All the boys gotta do cadets. We get dressed up and march about like soldiers and once a month we go shooting with old rifles — 303s.'

'What? Shooting what?'

'Targets, thick head. Though I'm hoping old Baldy'll pop up in front of one of them this year. Bang! Bull's-eye! He's the big boss of cadets.'

Jake looked at him, 'Do we get any time for work? School work?'

'Oh that. Sure do. You'n me and Maisie, Clare and Delma, we all do the same. Baldy teaches us English, history and geography. Dunno who'll be doing French, science and maths. If we're good enough we're allowed to sit School Cert this year instead of next year. Because I want to get out of this place before I'm an old man I'm sure as hell gonna be good enough this year,' said Robert.

'You want to get out of this place? Seems to me like you're the boss here.'

'Yeah, I am. But I'm ready for bigger things. Oh, one other thing.'

'What? You going to put me in the school choir, too?'

'We don't have one,' said Robert. 'Thank God. No. If we wanna smoke, and you need to if you go to this school, we go down by the river. It'll just be you and me, all the fourth form boys and one or two thirds who think they're grown up.'

'We could get caught.'

'Never. Look, mate, you seen our teachers. Most of 'em come to school in wheelchairs!'

'What about Lance?'

'Lance doesn't smoke but he sometimes comes down for a break. Not often. He's a genius, Lance. He lives for his maths and science and stuff and doesn't have a social life but he's OK. You can't blame him, his dad's the Presbyterian minister.'

'Have you put him in your cricket team?' Jake asked.

'Yep,' said Robert. 'He's one of the wickets.'

'Gibbons tells me you're doing rather well, lad,' James McGregor sipped his nightly whisky. 'You get on all right with the old codger?'

'Yes, when he's there. I think we teach ourselves most of the time.'

131

'Probably nothing too wrong with that, either.' He gave Jake a shrewd look. 'Tells me you've quite a brain. Maybe time to start giving a bit of thought to what might be done with it in the not too distant future.' He changed tack. 'Not a bad bowling arm, either, I hear. Better do my bit and come up and see the latter the next time you're in action. You've come a long way in, what is it? Nigh on a year?'

'Twelve thousand miles, Dr Mac.' Jake returned the smile.

'Don't get smart with me, laddie, I mean since you've been here with me. Put another log on the fire and pour yourself a wee dram.'

'I know what you mean.' Jake obeyed both instructions.

'Look at you. You've shot up a good half-head and filled out . . .'

'I'm not surprised,' said Jake. 'Between us we eat about a sheep a week!'

'Nothing wrong with that, either. And there's more to it than that. You're a good boy in spite of the company you keep.'

'Well, I know what they all say about you Dr Mac, but, to be honest, no one else has offered me a good home — and a sheep a week!'

James McGregor gave a full belly laugh. 'Quite a sly sense of humour, haven't we? Think I said that in my last note to your dad.'

'You write to my father?'

'Yes, boy. Once in while.'

'Really?'

'I don't tell lies, boy. Well, not too often.'

'I never knew.'

'Knew what? That I don't often tell lies or that I write to your old man?'

'I know about the lies. Didn't know about the other. D'you want a bit more whisky?'

'Thank you. And that's not an invitation for you to have another! It's getting a bit parky. Winter coming on far too quick.'

'Far too quickly, Dr Mac. Does my old man write back?' Jake was slightly defensive. 'He's not too good with words.'

'Bless you, boy. He does well enough. Now, a couple of things, laddie. I've business in Wellington in a couple of weeks. Thought I'd take you down so you can see the place. You'll miss a day or so of school but old Gibbons says that's neither here nor there. What d'you say?'

'It's a long way for me to drive,' said Jake, smiling.'

'Little devil. We'll catch the night train. Stay at the Midland, always put up there. I'll have Molly do me a list and we can get you kitted out a bit better.'

'It's about time I wrote to Dad again,' said Jake. 'May I have another whisky? To celebrate? Dear Dad, your son Jake, the young gentleman, is going to visit the capital of his new country.' He smiled broadly.

'You do me a world of good, boy, when you smile. Yes. Pour yourself the smallest of tots because now I'm afraid I've got to wipe that smile off your face.'

'What?' Apprehensive. 'What do you have to tell me?' No smile now.

'Pearson is out of borstal,' the doctor said. There was moment of silence. 'It was as well you knew.' Another moment. 'Don't look at me like that, Jacob. You'll be all right.' He looked at the boy and got to his feet. 'Come here. Come on. Come here,' and as Jake allowed himself to be comforted, the old man went on speaking. 'You'll like as not never see him. He'll keep his distance, you mark my words. If he knows what's good for him, that bastard will be keeping his nose clean.'

Jake was less certain.

As he lay in bed that night, sleep not coming, tossing, turning, muttering, 'Sooner or later, sooner or later, sooner or later,' half under his breath. 'Sooner or later he'll get me. Sooner or later, sooner or later . . .' He turned on his bedside lamp, but the glow brought no comfort. 'Sooner or later he'll come for me. Then what? This time he'll kill me . . .' As darkness turned to the grey light of early dawn, he fell into a fitful and half-wakeful sleep infested by scraps of nightmare with a cast of two; Darcy Pearson and Jacob Neill. Vengeful Pearson, bloodlust in his eyes. Neill cowering, waiting for the blow to fall.

Dragging himself from his tumbled bed and into the cold light of day, Jake prayed that whatever was to come would come sooner rather than later.

But, as day followed day and night followed night, nothing happened and the nightmares faded.

'Coming weekend in Wellington, laddie. Already told you about it. Time you saw our fine capital. Damn fool medical conference and the buggers want me to say something about country practice. Need to see the old legal eagles of mine, too. Kill two birds with one stone.'

'I don't think you're supposed to kill eagles, Dr Mac, not even the legal ones.'

'I'll kill whoever I like, boy.' The doctor smiled at him. 'Us quacks do, y'know. And I'll start with your damn cat unless it jumps off my lap. So, lad, what d'you say? Ready for the big smoke of Wellington?'

IX

'Seein' as we're doin' history, how're you getting on with Gary's lessons?' asked Robert, as they worked together on their homework at the Te Huia kitchen table.

'I haven't seen him for a while. He might've got his job down the city. Let's see — last time the Gestapo had me tied up in a cellar 'cos they caught me spying for Mr Churchill.'

'You?'

'Yes. Me.'

'Bull,' said Robert. 'I'm not Gary Miller! He believed you? Bullshit!'

'And I shall wash your mouth out with soap, young man,' said his mother. 'I won't have that foul language in this house. Stay away from Gary Miller, Jake. He's no better than that Pearson wretch. I can't understand you giving him the time of day, for all he might have apologised for what he did to you.'

'Aw, Mum. Gary's not that bad,' said her son.

'No. He's quite likely a deal worse. Now, feed the fire and boil that kettle — and then make a cup of tea. I want to hear all about Wellington from Jake. Robert tells me Mac took you to hear the National Orchestra. My word, you're a lucky boy. I'd give my eye teeth to go to something like that.'

'You could have had my seat,' he grinned. 'I went to sleep.'

'Tsk, tsk. Some people! And now, you two, another half hour of this history or whatever it is you're doing and then off home with you before Mac gets worried.'

'Dr Mac won't be worried. He's got the cop, Barry Jackson, and his new wife and Mrs Henderson all having dinner,' said Jake.

Jake and Robert spent three or four evenings a week studying together. There was a no nonsense approach to what they had to do. They didn't waste time. 'We do this, now,' said Robert, 'then we won't have to do it all at the last minute. Besides, I want to play serious footie. And so do you.'

'No I don't,' said Jake.

'Of course you do,' said Robert. 'You're a natural. Everyone says.'

'Like who? Who is there to say anything?'

'Well, that's what I say. It's what Maisie said, too, when she watched us play against Black River High.' He winked at Jake. 'She likes you, old Maisie. I can tell.'

'I don't know why, seeing as you gave me her place in the damn rugby team.'

'I was only joking,' said Robert.

Another half hour of European history and Jake got ready to leave. 'I'd come with you for the walk,' said Robert. 'But it's too cold and I haven't got any smokes and neither have you and there's a limit to my friendship.'

It was a still, cool night. Full moon and a touch of frost in the air. Jake had walked to the Te Huia home; his bike had a puncture and he hadn't got round to fixing it.

He took a shortcut, ducking down a rough alley between the pub and the post office, intending to cut across the empty site at the rear of the hotel. A five-minute walk.

The Weatherley Hotel did a brisk, back-door, after-hours liquor trade and the rear section provided handy private access and parking.

Jake huddled into his jacket and walked head down. He was almost across the wasteland when he spotted the truck. A warning registered in his mind but it was too late. The outer edges of his thinking took in the sight of the vehicle, the two or three figures lounging in the dim light around the deck of the truck, the clink of bottles. But it was almost the whole of his being that took in what confronted him. The bulky frame of Darcy Pearson.

'Now I've got you. Never thought it'd be this quick, this easy.' His familiar jeering voice. 'I've got you this time, Pongo. Jesus has answered all my prayers.' He snarled and lunged at Jake.

Jake, startled, started to turn, to run, to get away, but he was too late. No escape. With careless ease, Pearson's arm shot out and grabbed Jake, one hand around the boy's throat. An iron grip. Jake dropped his satchel and his books and papers scattered. 'I'll pay you back, you little bastard, for what you done to me.' He drew Jake towards him, shaking him, breathing beer fumes into his face. Pearson's eyes glittered in the moonlight. 'I've been dreaming of this for so long. Look at you! What are you? Nothing but useless pommy slime.'

Rabbit in a trap, mesmerised, terrified, its eyes on its captor, numb . . . Darcy Pearson held Jake slightly further away from him, shaking the boy, enjoying his strength and a rediscovered feeling of power. But the captor miscalculated. He'd been drinking.

'Couldn't take what was coming to you back then . . . you'll bloody take it now!' He shook Jake again. Darcy Pearson felt really good.

There was no way Jake could speak, say anything. Held in a vice-like grip it was hard enough to breathe much less make a sound. But Pearson had given him time to come out of his initial shock and back into at least a corner of his mind where he knew he had to do something to save himself. As Pearson wound himself into further fury, Jake did the only thing he could; he pulled back his right leg and kicked with every ounce of force and desperate strength in his body. His good solid shoe connected with Darcy Pearson's balls.

Two things happened. Pearson released Jake and Jake fell backwards onto the ground. Pearson crumpled, bent double, yelling in agony and clutching at himself.

Jake sprang to his feet as Pearson staggered upright, still groaning, still holding onto himself. Jake didn't give him a chance to recover. No thought, now, of flight! Every ounce of force that had gone into his foot was transferred to his fist and a right hook slammed into Darcy Pearson's jaw. Pearson dropped.

Jake became aware of Pearson's companions for the first time and recognised movement away from the truck and towards him. But it was only a slight recognition because one thing was uppermost in his mind. With his enemy prone at his feet all Jake wanted to do was to kill Darcy Pearson while he had the opportunity.

Screaming, now, at the top of his voice, Jake Neill gave vent to his pent up fury. Having started with a kick, first he went on booting, and then he sprang on the other as if possessed, straddling him and pummelling, punching, gouging . . . at one stage pulling Pearson's head up by his hair and bashing it two, three times, hard into the ground . . . 'You won't get me again you bloody bastard! You'll be dead! Bloody dead!' he gasped.

Jake had no perception that a further battle was now raging around him. Two of the three half-drunk mates of Darcy Pearson

138

tried to come to the rescue of their fallen comrade. The third, only slightly less drunk, held them at bay.

'He's killin' Darce!

'Gotta save Darce.'

'He's murderin' 'im!' and this one started to scream.

'Gotta let 'im do it,' yelled Gary Miller. 'Darce done it to him! Fair's fair,' and with relative ease he held the two strugglers away from the maniacal and one-sided encounter taking place on the ground in front of them.

Jake may well have killed Darcy Pearson. Yelling even louder in a high-pitched screaming wail that made no discernible sense, Jake now booted Pearson repeatedly, not caring where his kicks landed.

The yelling and the screaming probably saved Darcy Pearson and Jake Neill from dire consequences. As Jake's hand grabbed at a discarded beer bottle and he prepared to crown Darcy Pearson for good and all, two pairs of strong hands pulled him away. It took the combined strength of Robert Te Huia and the publican to hold Jake while Gary Miller and his two mates knelt at Darcy's side.

'Don' think he's dead 'cos he still doin' some breathin'. I think I can see some little wee breaths,' said Miller. 'Geez, old Darce's got a lot of blood in 'im. Well, it's not all in 'im, now.'

Jake pulled himself away from Robert and the publican. He was trembling, shivering, shaking. Wild-eyed and dishevelled, he stepped back and looked down at Pearson. 'I killed him! I killed him!' A triumphant yell, and then he looked at Robert. 'He'll never ever get me again!' He blinked, and then the enormity of his actions started to sink in. 'Bugger off! Leave me alone,' he yelled, and ran off into the darkness.

X

Jake burst into James McGregor's sitting-room. Clutching onto the door, he yelled at Dr Mac and Barry Jackson, the policeman, as they enjoyed a last nightcap. 'I got that bastard! I killed that bastard! You can arrest me now.' And he held out two hands.

The noise brought the two women through from the kitchen, Molly Henderson hastily wiping dry her hands on a tea towel. 'He's dead now,' Jake's lip trembled. 'Stone dead. He's out the back of the pub on the ground. Dead. You can take me. He won't get me now and I don't care if I get hanged.' And then he crumpled.

Molly Henderson moved towards Jake. 'Leave him,' said James McGregor, quietly. 'Leave him to me.'

'I'd better go and have a look,' said Barry Jackson. 'Back of the pub? Hmm. Yet again! Young Pearson, I imagine. I'm picking he's not dead.' He wore a small and wintry smile. 'I'll be back — or I'll phone. Come on, love,' he said to his wife, and they left.

'No, Molly. I'll see to this one,' James McGregor said firmly. 'You take off now.'

'Are you sure . . . '

'Yes. Quite sure.'

'Get up, lad,' said the doctor. 'Can't bend down there. Here,' he held out a glass. 'Have a sip of this. Not whisky, the cop's drunk me out of it. Drop of brandy.'

'I've killed him,' Jake muttered, taking the glass.

'We won't talk about it now. You got anything broken?'

Jake shook his head. 'I don't think so. No.'

James McGregor looked at the boy. 'Then, finish your drink, go wash yourself up and then get to your room for half an hour or so. Then both of us might be ready to talk.'

'Don't want to talk.'

'You'll do as you're told,' said Dr McGregor. 'Be off with you.'

The doctor answered the phone. 'I take it he's not dead?' Pause. 'Bit of a pity.' Another pause. 'You don't want me to open up the surgery? Good. I'll see him in the morning, then.' Pause, slight smile. 'Good idea. I'll fix him up while you have a chat to the lad. Sorry it wrecked an otherwise pleasant evening. Hmm. Inevitable, I guess.'

James McGregor went to Jake's room.

Jake sat on the far corner of his bed, his back to the wall, knees up to his chin and arms hugging his legs.

'Tell me about it,' said James McGregor, and he sat on the bottom of the bed.

'Nothing to tell. I killed him.'

'Nonsense. I'm told he's battered and bruised, but otherwise he's all there.'

'I wanted him dead. I wanted to kill him. I tried to kill him.'

'I'm sure you did.'

'Is the cop coming back to get me? Is he going to arrest me?'

'I doubt it. The cop, young man, is the least of your worries,' said the doctor.

'What do you mean?'

'Getting into a brawl with that scum, you could have been seriously hurt yourself. Worse, even. Why? For what?'

'He attacked me.' His voice was sullen.

'I don't doubt it. I don't want to know the details. Clearly you gave the blighter a thrashing. Clearly you let yourself be reduced to his level. I trust you're satisfied. You're now one with him. Happy? Eh?' James McGregor did not relent.

'You don't know what happened.'

'I can guess. Somehow or other you got the bugger down. Somehow or other you had him in your power. And somehow or other, young man, there was a moment when you should have cut and bloody run; got the hell out of it. You didn't!' He stood. 'You, young man, you . . . your behaviour disgusts me!' The old man's fury intensified.

Jake stood up, away from the bed, looked the doctor in the eye, and yelled. 'You saw what he did to me. You can still see what he bloody did to me, it'll always be there. He would've done it again. That bloody bastard would have bloody done it again!'

'Moderate your bloody language, sir!' James McGregor breathed heavily. 'You reduce yourself to a gutter level. Violence! You don't know the meaning of the word and you know less where it leads, where it ends up. I thought, given your sad background, that was one lesson you'd never have to learn from an old bastard like me. Sit down! Don't you stand there as if threatening me! Sit, sir!'

Jake sat. He ground his teeth, glared at the old man, said nothing.

'You came here, God knows how, all those months ago, as wretched a scrap of humanity as I've seen in one hell of a long time. Bewildered, bemused, lost, in pain. The hurt in your eyes told it all in a way that took me back a long time to times I try not to remember and the three years or more I spent patching up young men, little older than you are now, who had taken worse than they ever deserved, worse than they had ever dreamed of . . . The other great war, laddie . . . and their eyes looking up at me, telling me they had not the foggiest notion of why it had happened to them.'

'I don't think . . . ' Jake started.

'I'm talking, lad. And there is not the slightest need to tell me you don't think. I know you didn't think.'

'I didn't . . .'

'Be quiet. If I learnt one thing, all those years ago . . . one lesson that remains with me to this day, and will until the day I die, is that the end product of violence is more violence . . . I'll say it again; violence begets violence! If suffering humanity is to have any chance of survival we must find better ways to live with each other and our differences,' James McGregor's voice lowered and he sat again. 'I thought, Jacob, lad, that you might have absorbed a little more of that philosophy by living here with me.' He looked at the boy. 'I'm not blind, you know. I've watched, observed and approved of how you seem to have patched up matters with that other brute who abused you, young Miller. I'll never like the oaf, but I do give him, and you, full credit for however you managed what must have been a difficult transition. That is behaviour I admire. Maybe I should have told you so at the time. The other way, Jake, fills me with despair, dismay . . .' He sighed deeply.

For a half minute or more the young man and the old man looked at each other, eyes locked. It was Jake who broke the silence. He stood and looked down at James McGregor and said, 'I'm not threatening you because I'm standing up,' he spoke quietly, politely. 'I think I must leave now,' and he walked over to his wardrobe, opened the door and pulled down from the top shelf his battered

143

cardboard suitcase. 'I'll pack my things. I can leave school because I'm fifteen.'

'Where will you go?' Said quietly, with the very faintest of smiles.

'Wellington. It's a good place. I like it.'

'Oh, yes. What will you do there?'

'I'll get a job. I can work.'

'I know that,' said James McGregor. 'Ample proof of that, every day.'

'I'll have to take the clothes you got me but I'll pay you back when I can. All my things are gone except my jacket and that doesn't fit any more. Molly said I should keep that as a reminder and she used the rest of my things for dusters.' And even more quietly. 'I'm sorry I disgust you. I wouldn't ever want to disgust you. Thank you for all you've done for me, but I can't be any better than what I am. Shit, I don't want to cry . . .'

The old man didn't move to comfort the boy. He just sat there with his eyes on him, still wearing a faint smile.

'I disgust you. I can't stand that, not after all you've done.' Jake hung his head.

The doctor finally spoke. 'Sit down, laddie. Wipe your eyes and your nose. Here.' He held out a handkerchief. 'I have not the slightest intention of going back on anything I've said other than to point out one quite important detail . . .'

'What's that?'

'I did not say that you disgusted me, Jacob.'

'Yes, you did.'

'Stop interrupting me, boy. You don't disgust me. You should bloody listen. I told you that your behaviour disgusted me. Your action disgusted me. Think about what I said. Sweet lad, you've

144

grown to fill my life with a great deal of joy, much happiness and more than a little laughter. I watch you grow into a fine and good young man and I am delighted. You repay me in so many ways for what was quite likely a nonsense notion of thinking a doddery old fool could do something for someone else who, God knows, surely needed something done for them! Put your bloody suitcase back in its cupboard. There will come a day when you have to pack it, but it's not now.'

'But . . . '

'But nothing. I said what had to be said. I've had serious words with you. You have no option but to allow me that. It's not a privilege on my part. It's a responsibility. I make absolutely no apology. You did wrong. It's my job, whether you like it or not, to point out what I see as the error of your ways. You're going nowhere, except to the kitchen to make us a cup of tea. This is your home, Jake. For right or wrong, this is your home. It continues to be your home no matter how many strips I am forced to tear from you! Do you understand?'

'Yes I do,' said Jake, head bowed. The two of them sat, not touching, side by side on Jake's bed. 'But I do have to say one thing if I'm to be honest with you.'

'What's that?'

'If what happened tonight, the situation, if it happened again . . . '

'Yes.'

'I can't promise you that I wouldn't do the same thing again, no matter how hard I tried not to. If that bastard was in front of me, I would still want to kill him. I know I would.'

'That's understandable.'

'I can promise I'd do my best to remember to think of alternatives but . . .'

145

'Probably the most I can ask of you, at this stage,' said James McGregor, wryly, his smile growing a little. 'I suppose, in the light of what you say, I should pray that, next time, and I hope a next time never happens, the boot continues to be on the same foot! Let me just remind you, regardless of what I say, I have not the tiniest scrap of sympathy for Pearson. None at all. I am sure you dealt to him only a fraction of what he deserved.' The old man's small smile spread into a broad grin and his face was that of a boy. 'I imagine it felt good!'

'I think it did at the time. Must have done because I went on hammering him. But I don't know, not really. Not now. Now I just have an empty feeling.'

'I'm very glad to hear that.' The doctor stood and smiled down at Jake. 'Means you're not totally beyond redemption. Come on. Cup of tea. We both need one. And then you had better get to bed.'

'Shake hands,' said Jake, and extended his hand.

'Certainly. But not too hard. Now I know the power of that fist I could be in significant danger!'

'I've got to tell you this, Jake. You're lucky, bloody lucky I'm not here to take you in!' said Barry Jackson. 'Mac tells me he's made his point to you, well and truly, so there's not much need to say more.'

Jake and the constable sat in a sheltered corner of the veranda. Molly Henderson had brought them tea and scones, and left them to it. 'What did I do to him?'

'Probably less than you intended. Murder may have been on your mind but he's going to live. He's with his mother, getting a spot of attention and, I imagine, not too tender care! Possibly a cracked rib or two, minus a front tooth, a very sore jaw, various swollen bits and pieces in sensitive areas and, I would think, a headache like he's never had before.' He gave a slight chuckle. 'Nothing too serious.'

'Why aren't you going to arrest me?'

'Well, you see, I can only agree with what Dr Mac said to you up to a point,' said Barry Jackson. He took out his cigarettes, lit one, offered the pack to Jake.

'Thanks,' said Jake.

The policeman spoke very quietly. 'I don't care who takes on that brute or what they do to him. To my mind it would always be less than he deserved. Violence may never solve anything but that is a good and simple message that never gets through to the likes of Pearson. I know this is different from what Dr Mac has told you and I'm not going against anything he might have said. Understand?'

'Yes.'

'You're a tough little blighter. I've watched you play football. Guess you've had to be over the years, getting through everything you've had to face. I've also watched you recover from what Pearson did to you — and I will never forget what he did and how you looked. You pulled yourself back together in fine fashion, my man, and you can be proud of yourself for that. Never looked for sympathy and, as far as I know, never whined and moaned about your lot.'

'I think I did,' Jake gave a small smile. 'You should ask Dr Mac and Molly.'

'It would have killed me to have had to arrest you for last night. Believe me. You came within a hair's breadth of booting the brains out of the sod. You know that? Now, given the history of all this, while you might not have been found guilty of murder, it would have been manslaughter and a long time behind bars! Understand?'

'Yes.'

'God knows how, but you seem to have something of a friend in Gary Miller. He told me the ins and outs of the whole shooting match. Which reminds me, I had no idea you'd been an undercover agent for Churchill. Remarkable life you've led!'

Jake grinned and looked at the policeman. 'Yes, I have.'

'He's not worth it, Jake. Pearson, I mean.'

'I know that,' said Jake. 'Look,' he floundered. 'Look, it won't happen again. I promise. I said to Dr Mac that I couldn't promise what I would do if the same thing cropped up another time . . . but I think I can say it won't. When I think about it, even though I wouldn't want to, I'd run.'

'Well, then, good,' said Barry Jackson. 'Enough said.'

'I've got to tell you though . . . I did want to kill him.'

'Fair enough, on the one hand. Bloody stupid on the other. He's not worth the mess you'd find yourself in. You may be pleased to know that Pearson is in considerably more trouble than you.'

'How come?'

'Well, he's on a sort of parole. Got out of borstal double quick on account of his old man needing him on the farm. And ask yourself . . . what's he doing buying beer, under age and after hours? Pearson's meant to be safely at home tucked up secure in his little bed during the hours of darkness. Don't you worry, Jake, he's got some very hard talking to do, that one, and at the end of the day will be lucky not to be back in borstal for another six months or so. If my word's worth anything, that's where he's headed.'

Jake's broad smile said it all.

'I thought that would please you,' said the policeman.

'Robert and me once planned how we were going to hang Darcy Pearson.'

'I bet it was going to be very painful.'

'Sure was. We were going to stretch his neck very, very slowly.'

'Robert tells me you're a crack shot on the old bunnies. How about you and him coming with me one weekend to chase a few deer up in the foothills? That's my favourite sport. Mind you, these days I've got to get permission from my better half, and that's not always easy.' Jackson smiled.

'That'd be great, thank you.'

'I know old Mac isn't that hot on violence and all that but I happen to know he does enjoy a nice roast of venison. The damn things are taking over up there, so we can call it a public service. Now I'd better get on my way. Got a rather sticky interview with the good folks at the pub!'

'Thank you for everything.'

'Nothing to thank me for, Jake.'

'Could I thank you for another cigarette before you go?'

'Don't press your luck, boy. Buy your own!' and Barry Jackson took his pack from his pocket. 'I know Mac has told you that while he's pretty damned disappointed at what you did, he does understand what drove you to do it. We agree on that. We also agree that should it happen again, for God's sake, run like the bloody clappers! You know what you're up against and you've the sense and wit to know that a character like Pearson hasn't heard of the Marquess of Queensberry and you're likely to have a broken beer bottle shoved in your face.' He looked at Jake for a moment. 'Mind you, boy, I wasn't too sure after I had a look at the sod that you'd heard of the good Marquess, either!'

Jake Neill stood on the veranda in the wintery sun, his cat, Big Black Sambo, sitting beside him, surveying his territory. Jake's steel-grey eyes were hard and cold as he watched, taking in Darcy Pearson's every pained movement as he hobbled, aided by his mother, from the doctor's surgery. Pearson stopped to rest for a moment and caught sight of Jake. Their two eyes locked. Nothing was said. Mrs Pearson pointedly looked in the opposite direction.

Satisfied at what he'd seen, Jake turned and walked into the house. Big Black Sambo stayed where he was.

XI

My dear son Jacob

Thank you for the telegram that come on the same day as your Christmas parcel which was a month late but that is O.K. Two Christmasses you been gone now. Time flies. I was pleased to here you got this school cert not that I know what it is but I work out is the exams you have had and passed. This is good and you are a credit. The good doctor must be proud of you like me. Might be one day you will be a doctor and that would be handy for me ha ha. But I do not know. It takes a lot of time I feel sure and I think you will go to work now. You are old enough and with an exam like you got can get a job at the factory where you are that makes all that butter and you can make good money. What say you?

I must say it is good to know you are fine. I must say it is not good I never know about Janny. Not one word if she is live or if she is dead. It is like I never had a girl and at times it gets me down when I think of it. But then I think it is better off for her where she lives and if she gets to write in a year or so when she knows how that is fine. It's a funny old world ha ha.

The new job in the box factory is fine and I don't
have to stand all the time. This is long for me and I shall
stop now. I like your letters. You are the clever one.

Give my wishes to the doctor and to Mrs Molly.
On a wing and a prayer (one leg and a prayer ha ha)
Your Dad X.

'Never seen that red dahlia flower so well. What've you done to it, lad?' asked James McGregor, surveying a bank of blooms.

'I just did as you told me.' Jake pointed. 'That whole lot there got God knows how many wheelbarrows of horse shit in spring.'

'Manure,' said Mac.

'That's what I said,' grinned Jake. 'It would have been easier to get one of next-door's horses, tie it up in the garden and tell it to get to work. That horse *manure*,' he stressed the word, 'near broke my back!'

'Nonsense. Damned good exercise, and it's worked a treat,' said the doctor. 'The place is looking good, boy. You've done well. Let's have a look at the pond. My favourite spot. A good garden, Jacob, is balm for the soul.'

'But not for the back.'

'Stop moaning, boy. From what I see, you enjoy every moment of it and get as much enjoyment out of the old place as I do. Go fetch a bottle of beer from the house. Hot work this gardening.'

'Well,' said Jake. 'It is for one of us!'

They settled down and drank their beer by the lily pond, enjoying the warmth of the summer evening.

'You miss your old man, don't you?' James McGregor asked.

'Yes,' Jake thought for a moment. 'Why d'you ask just now?'

'I know you had a letter, lad. The smile is not quite as bright?'

'Well, he was all Janice and me had when everything was over. Funny in a way. He was the one sent us away, didn't he?'

'For the best possible reasons, lad. There was your future, and that of the little one, your sister, to think of. And how was he, poor man, to care for the two of you?'

'I know all that. I know he did it for the best. But we didn't ask to be sent away. Not that he knew it, but he sent me to bloody hell, didn't he? And I don't know where Janice is. I'll never know where Janice is,' Jake was silent for a moment. 'It was sheer good luck I ended up here with someone who . . . well, cares for me and, I think, well . . . likes me.'

'Go on, laddie, you can say it,' the old man chuckled. 'Someone who loves you, is what you wanted to say.'

'Don't put words in my mouth, Dr Mac.' Jake smiled at his friend.

'Do you miss the old country?'

'England? Hell no!' Very firm. 'Not ever. OK, so I'm English and I don't hate the place but I didn't have much of a life there, did I? Look at everything I have now. I'd never have that at home. I'd be working by now, probably somewhere like the box factory my dad works in. I wouldn't be still at school. I know I'm lucky, bloody lucky, this is my home.'

James McGregor looked hard at Jake. 'Thank you for saying that, boy. That's the first time I've heard you put it that way. It is your home. It always will be. Pour me another beer. Go get another bottle. I'm thirsty.'

Jake brought back two more bottles. 'In case you're very thirsty,' and he laughed. 'You think about it. Think of what, thanks to you, I can do here. I'm still at school. I live in this grand place with a grand old gentleman,' he winked broadly at James McGregor. 'A

153

grand old bad-tempered gent who drinks too much beer, but I can ignore that . . .'

'Yes. You'd better, if you want to go on drinking your share of his beer!'

'Robert and me are going to play golf this year. His uncle's got it all jacked-up. There's no way I could even dream of that at home. I play rugby. Wouldn't ever do that at home,' he smiled broadly. 'God, if I was lucky I might get to boot some sissy round ball on a flattened bomb site! Got everything here. Barry even takes us deer stalking in the hills . . .'

'As nice a bit of venison as I've ever tasted, that last one.'

'Should've been. Not much more than a poor little baby, but it didn't suffer,' said Jake. 'But above all, because of you, I seem to be able to do whatever I want to do. He grinned. 'And even if it is only Weatherley District High, I'm getting an education.'

'You're getting that through no effort of mine, lad. It's your hard work paying off. Great results. Which brings me to the point, young man.'

'What point?'

'What's this damn fool notion of yours Molly's told me about?'

'I don't know what you mean,' said Jake, looking the other way.

'Don't lie to me, sir.'

Jake turned back to face the doctor and blushed bright red beneath his summer tan. 'I didn't want to tell you. Not yet.'

'Not yet? When, then? After you'd fully qualified. Didn't cross your mind I'd get a mite suspicious as the years rolled by; not suspect anything until the glorious day you turned up on the doorstep, your little suitcase in hand and a brand-new stethoscope dangling round your neck?'

'I want to be a doctor,' said Jake.

'Over my dead body,' said Dr Mac.

'You can't stop me,' said Jake.

'I can give it a damn good try,' said Dr Mac. 'Why, for God's sake? Is it simply because you're living here with an old nitwit who didn't have the sense to make a better choice when he was your age?'

'Yep,' said Jake. 'Something like that.'

'We will talk more of this, boy,' said James McGregor. 'Help me up. The sun's shed its last rays for the day. A bloody doctor? Fiddlesticks and phooey! As if one in the family weren't enough. Mind you,' he chuckled. 'Rate I'm degenerating, there may be no need to worry on that count. Only ever be one in the damn family! Come on!' he ordered.

EARLY SUMMER 1950

The tall young man lounged against the car, finding little to enjoy in this one spot he hated more than any other place. The sun shone, but, even so, he shivered slightly in its pleasant warmth. He lit a cigarette and turned so he faced away from the old man who clumped up and down the pot-holed asphalt strip behind him. He checked his watch and muttered a curse, 'Bloody train had to be bloody late today, of all bloody days!' He felt even sorrier for himself. The old man wandered off and leaned against a fence a hundred yards or more away. He examined a crop of swedes.

Jake began to pace what passed for a platform and, as always when he came to this place, failed to rid his mind of the image of a much smaller boy, alone and frightened, in a Harris tweed jacket with his small, battered suitcase beside him.

'No, Mac. Please, Mac,' he'd pleaded. 'Not today. It's my last match for the school. The last one, ever! Pukeonake High, and maybe this time we'll beat the sods. Gotta be there, I'm the captain, for God's sake! Please. Can't you phone your friend and ask him to make it later in the week?' It was bound to be old Judge Freddie again, coming for a few days of fishing, of swapping yarns and drinking Mac's whisky.

'Impossible, laddie.'

'Barbara can drive you.'

'Barbara's off and away. You know as well as I do she's doing a stint up at the hospital while old Lil's down country doing what she can to learn what it takes to be a nurse in the second half of the century. Bloody miracle needed there!'

'Molly? Hell's bells, Mac, all she's doing is painting that other bedroom that doesn't even need it.'

'Molly's up to her eyeballs in . . . No, lad. Afraid it's got to be you. Let that be an end to the matter,' brooking no argument. 'Sorry about your jolly game, but I'm sure there's a way around an hour or so of your absence. Do your best to see it's your team gets to bat on Thursday. Cheat, if you have to. Get your mate Robert on to it. He'll talk a way around it, if anyone can. No one is one hundred percent indispensable. Not even you.'

Life was quietening for the old man. Early in the New Year he would take on a younger partner. 'She'll be doing the legwork, the house calls, the hospital. Just be keeping enough to myself to keep my hand in and stay alive.'

'Reckon she'll do the lawns and gardens?' Jake had asked.

'May be stretching it a bit far. But that side of it's not my worry, young man. You want to walk out on me, it's your job to find a suitable replacement before you take off. Whoever you find had better be bloody good.'

'I feel sorry for them already,' Jake smiled. 'Don't worry. I'll find the poor little sod and train him well before I go.' He looked at his old friend. 'You know . . . you've only got to say *don't go* and I won't.'

The doctor gave a chuckle. 'Put that way, Jacob, you don't really give me much option, do you? Of course you'll be going, boy. It's the way of things. I hate to say it, but, you'll make a damn fine doctor one of these days. Dammit. Would have wished you'd chosen otherwise, but . . . I'll be doing what I can to help you along the way.'

'Yeah. No need for you to be helping me quite as much as you will be doing,' Jake was serious. 'Robert and me had it all planned. Him and me were going to go deer-culling for the government for a year or so, make a fortune, then varsity. Do us good. The great outdoors, and all that.'

'Stuff and nonsense,' said James McGregor. 'Pleases me more to have the noses of the two of you planted firmly to the academic grindstone than have you frisking and frolicking around the bush making life a misery for innocent deer or shooting each other. And don't you be thinking it's solely on your account I'll be helping that grinning monkey, too. Been planned for years.'

'I know that,' said Jake.

'Neither you nor he have been the first, and, with any luck won't be the last. One thing the old girl and I decided on many moons ago,' and he looked towards the photograph of himself and his wife. 'Nothing else to do with the damned stuff.'

'I just want to say . . .' Jake began.

'Well, don't,' Mac held up a hand. 'You've said it all, Jake. Many times over. You've given me as much, more, than I've given you. I know full well what you show me in everything you do for me. There is only one more thing you can do for me.'

'What? Another whisky?'

'Simply never forget that this is your home.'

Jake smiled. 'I know it always will be that.'

'Oh, yes, mister, you're right on the button there. In the fullness of time it will be yours in a practical sense,' he looked at Jake. 'Don't bother floundering around groping for the right word, young man. Enough said! Is that clear?' He glared at Jake. 'Now you can pour me another tot.'

Jake said nothing.

James McGregor finished his scrutiny of the crop of swedes. 'Thought I heard it. Come on, laddie.'

The plumes of smoke and steam rose above the low hills and the train came into view around the last bend. 'Just hope to God the guard hasn't lost old Freddie's fishing rods this time,' Jake yelled.

'Freddie? What was that about . . .' the rest of the doctor's words were lost as the train roared, hissed, slowed. The old man hobbled off along the platform, leaving Jake behind him.

The train stopped. Jake glanced along the line of carriages to see from which Dr Mac's guest would alight. For a moment or two, nothing. 'He'll be in the last bugger. Always is. And slower than a bloody snail,' Jake muttered, peering through the cloud of wafting smoke and steam. He saw the guard jump down and turn to the steps of the carriage to help a small figure, a child, jump down before turning back to assist someone else.

Jake began to walk towards James McGregor. And then he froze. Absolutely stock-still. 'No,' he yelled. 'No!' louder. 'It can't be . . . it isn't . . .' and his hand came up to cover his mouth and he began to tremble. 'Oh Jesus God it is . . .' and he began to run. 'My dad . . . my dad . . . and it's Janny. Janny! Janny!' he yelled. 'Daddy . . . Dad . . .' a scream torn from his whole being. 'It's me. It's your Jake! Here I am.'

AUTHOR'S NOTE

During the first half of the twentieth century, most particularly after World War II, many British children were sent to New Zealand, Australia, Canada and South Africa to find 'new and better homes'. Some 5000 children were sent to Australia and around 750 to New Zealand after the Second World War. A general term for these children was 'war orphans'. While a number of these children were orphans, many were not.

Sometimes the 'new life' was better. Sometimes it was not. As recent inquiries have shown, often the transition was a painful one, and instances of abuse were commonplace; both institutionally and at the hands of individuals and families. Too often the children were seen as little more than a source of labour, often on farms. Farm help, cheap or expensive, was hard to find during this period.

It is also true to say that most of these children were actively encouraged to sever all ties with their homelands and families. That so many did achieve success and eventually find happiness and security in their new lives is to their credit. Our society stands in their debt.